THE LONGEST WOODEN RAILROAD

A Season of Embers

For
Mark,
Hope you enjoy the story

David C. Hascall RN

12/21/14

THE LONGEST WOODEN RAILROAD

A Season of Embers

David C. Hascall

THE LONGEST WOODEN RAILROAD
A SEASON of EMBERS

Copyright © 2012 by David C. Hascall

All rights reserved.

ILLUSTRATIONS BY Philip Chancey

COVER DESIGN by Randall Beiderwell

EDITING BY Jeff and Marlie Moses, and Barbara B Gleason

Library of Congress Cataloging-in-Publication Data
Hascall, David C. (1949 –   )
The Longest Wooden Railroad
by David C. Hascall. —First edition.
ISBN: 978-0-9824441-8-4
1. Railroads. 2. Oregon.

PUBLISHED BY CRANEDANCE PUBLICATIONS
PO Box 50535, Eugene OR 97405
(541) 345-3974 • www.cranedance.com

PRINTING HISTORY
First edition: March 2013

Printed in the United States of America

DEDICATION

For Barbara, my wife and best friend.

—David C. Hascall

Epigraph

A good novel tells the truth about its hero;
but a bad novel tells us the truth about its author.

—G. K. Chesterton

FOREWORD

The Horton railroad, the longest railroad ever built with wooden rails instead of iron, would still be in existence today had a supply of rock been available to use as ballast under the rails. If it would still be operational, hauling logs out of the Lake Creek Valley is another matter. However, even the creative use of sturdy trestle pilings in place of crushed rock could not preserve the line's existence, in the face of fire, and the inevitable decay of things made entirely of wood. It is the way of things in the forest. I wrote, *No Way to ~~Run~~/Build a Railroad* in 1991, to preserve the memory of the community of people who built the line, their unique bit of railroad history and to correct the ridicule heaped upon the builders. In my research, I found nothing I could fault these people for.

No other incidents in the progress of civilization that I am familiar with presented more obstacles facing the participants. And yet, left with a choice, of their own volition they continued on. Why? Simply put: they had pioneering perseverance, just like the generation before them. After fourteen months of searching records, I felt I knew these people as well as anyone. They deserved better than they got. Should they not have even tried to build the railroad without rock for ballast, when they had other raw materials all around them? Even a failed railroad has a place in Oregon history.

David Hascall has written a fictional story of the railroad builders living in Horton in 1929. His interest in the railroad goes back farther than 2005, when he first contacted me.

Both of us agree this group of people—sons, daughters, kinfolk of pioneers, homesteaders, farmers, loggers, and mill owners—were all hard working honest people. They were the backbone, heart and soul of rural America. Later these same people were to become known as "The Greatest Generation."

I had not the slightest inkling of another story such as David has written, both in the same era and setting. I had no qualms at all accepting the fact that the women in the involved families, had, with some degree of reluctance, acquiesced (to) their spouse's participation in the project. Even so, women didn't just step in and grab the bull by the horns. They didn't do men's work if they had a large family. There just wasn't enough time in the day. Women were readily permitted to teach school. I suspect Mr. Hascall knows one or more teachers. In remote areas such as Horton, teachers were the source of knowledge and information.

My dear wife commented after her review of the manuscript, by saying, "What an interesting story."

"How does it compare to my "true" story," which took me fourteen months to research and write," I asked?

"Maybe you didn't take enough time to write yours."

So much for critics. Go ahead and read *The Longest Wooden Railroad, A Season of Embers*. You may like the story, too. I think it would make a good movie.

–Earl Kelley, author of No Way to <s>Run</s> / Build a Railroad

PREFACE

I met with Earl Kelley only once.

In his lifetime, Earl had worn many hats: he had been a successful building contractor, but also prided himself on being an author, a word warrior. Occasionally unpopular, he smiled as he recalled the events that stirred things up a bit.

I brought curiosity and a notebook to his living room in Florence, Oregon. Having come to interview him, I soon realized it was his interview to direct, not mine.

I sat facing a man that seemed to closely resemble those people he was asking me to write about. He was dressed for work, in fitted slacks and matching shirt. A pair of editor's dark rim glasses accented his strong, resolute, thin frame.

His living room—turned office—was walled in dark paneling with open ceiling beams, warmed by a wood stove. Family pictures and awards hung on the walls. His research on various subjects was stacked around him in an order known only to him. The only sign of slowing down after eighty years, was a slight shuffle in his step as he retreated to his stuffed chair—now his throne. His handshake was firmer than I expected and he definitely had my attention.

"I've been waiting for someone to pick this story up," he said, "and you're it." I sat dumbfounded, like a newspaper cub on his first assignment: listening, taking notes, drinking his coffee, and nodding at his instructions. There were people he wanted me to talk to, and a map he had made, tracing the route of the longest railroad ever made using wooden rails instead of iron. He asked me not to drop in on folks that I planned to interview. "Call ahead and request an invitation," Earl insisted.

After two hours it was over, and we exchanged gifts. My gift to him was a T-shirt from the Horton Store. His gift to me was a signed copy of his book, "*No Way to ~~Run~~/Build a Railroad: The Arnold, Junction City, Horton Auto Rail Company.*" Inside, he had written a note:

> *Thank you for the Horton Shirt.*
> *Happy you liked the story.*
> > *Earl L Kelley*

He had spent fourteen months going through old records and writing a story about the longest railroad ever built to run on wooden tracks, which seemed more like fiction than fact.

I first learned about the Horton Railroad in 1972, while helping Richard Winston, a graduate student at the University of Oregon, find the Horton Railroad grade. Since then, I hadn't been able to shake the feeling that there was something more that needed to be unearthed. That opportunity came when Earl shared what he knew during our interview in 2005 and asked me tell the rest of the story. So, who were these people and what were their lives about in 1929? And, what happened to this railroad? Why did it fail?

It has been a few years since that fateful encounter, but I had other dreams. I did the research, and just as he instructed, I walked the grade, following his map, and interviewed great men still living along the Horton Railroad grade. These men had so much pride, not just in the Horton Railroad that they watched being built from 1925-1929, but in what they had accomplished afterwards. These sons of pioneers also had other dreams, and a vision as great as their pioneer fathers.

I left Earl Kelley's home with a few of the artifacts that he had gathered over the years and carefully laid out and displayed in his carport. To this day I still have a few of the rusting iron nails, along with pieces of rotting hemlock planks. The wood no longer resembles the original 2 X

8 inch laminated boards that had been fitted together to construct the wooden track, but I can't bear to throw away any of these historic relics. When I look at them now, old memories return.

Growing up in a small mill town in the Oregon Coast Range, I remember all the sounds: the sawmill whistle at dawn, the drone of the saw blades cutting slabs of wood from each log, and the planer smoothing the rough-cut boards. I can still feel the intense heat from the four-story tall wigwam burner, an inferno in a cone-shaped tower with rusted metal sides that glowed orange from burning sawdust and other wood debris. There are still a few burners standing, if you know where to look. I always hurried past the chorus of unseen bullfrogs around the log pond at sunset. You rarely saw them, but you knew they were there.

When the timber was gone, the mill workers moved on from my home town of Vernonia, Oregon. An ingenious plan developed for the abandoned mill, which became a movie set for the Hollywood movie, Ring of Fire. The mill was burned to the ground, providing a dramatic ending to the movie. Fire in this case had some redeeming value for the town; not so for the community of Horton.

The reader is directed to the author's book web site (see below) for additional information including portions of my recent reunion with Earl Kelley, a brief audio portion of the book and video footage of the operation of a steam powered saw mill, similar to the one that operated in Horton. Website url: www.longestwoodenrailroad.com

The Horton Railroad holds a unique status in history, yet little is known about the people who built it, their lives, their loves, or their struggles. One can tell that the people in Horton who were living at the time, and who are willing to talk about the railroad, still have strong feelings. Even today they remember the stories of ridicule that the community received over the money lost in the venture. In walking the grade, however, one feels a presence in the wind and trees, as if gentle voices are asking for their story to be finished.

David Hascall The Longest Wooden Railroad

INTRODUCTION

This book is about the longest wooden railroad ever built and about a community of entrepreneurs in the 1920s, both men and women, who envisioned the future of timber and wood products as a resource on a par with farming. This had previously not been the case in agricultural Oregon and its Willamette Valley. Land was usually cleared to make way for growing wheat, vegetables, grass seed, fruit trees, and ranching.

Building a shortcut railroad to move timber to market, however, made sense at that time and in retrospect, since within ten years, by 1938, Oregon produced more lumber than any other state in the union. Today, timber continues to be logged and transported by logging truck rather than by rail from the Oregon Coast Range around Horton, Oregon.

While we cannot put the wooden railroad project alongside other pioneering accomplishments of this era, like the Lindbergh flight across the Atlantic, Women's Suffrage, or Admiral Byrd's journey to the North and South Poles, we can note that these people possessed a similar pioneer spirit like the adventurers of the time. It must have seemed quite normal to follow in the footsteps of their fathers and mothers who gambled to cross the plains in covered wagons or who dared to give women the right to vote.

There were doubters at every turn. And, like so many accomplishments recorded in history, if you gambled and won, you won big, but if you lost, you also lost big. The Horton Railroad is an example of the latter. Ridicule serves no purpose.

Suspicions often fell less on the project than on outsiders who promised quick profits and steady income. Belonging to a community still resonates today, as the first question often asked when meeting new acquaintances is: "Where are you from?" We take pride and perspective by answering that simple question.

For a review of the factual existence of the wooden-railed railroad built in Oregon between the town of Horton and Territorial Highway near Junction City, the reader is referred to Earl Kelley's excellent historical account, *No Way to Run/Build a Railroad*, self-published in 1991. He was gracious enough to write the foreword for this work.

Pieces of one of the locomotives serving this rail line can still be seen in the back yard of the Junction City Historical Museum. In addition, a rail car likely used on the line is parked along Territorial Highway two miles south of Monroe, Oregon.

Interviews I conducted of the old-timers, men living along the wooden rails at either end of the grade, validated the existence of the railroad for me as well, adding their sense of pride in the accomplishment of building sixteen miles of wooden tracks through the Oregon Coast Range.

Women were on the move in the 1920s! Having received the right to vote in Oregon in 1912, social roles were disrupted by World War I and the reality that women, around the world, could perform equally well in the work force previously dominated by men. While in some rural areas women remained limited to nursing or school teaching outside the home, many saw a "Rosie the Riveter" vision for the future and were eager to spread the news. In the 1920s some of these women were called Flappers.

Dissatisfied with the work world they entered, women's desire for better working conditions and benefits at home served as a foundational starting point for multiple social welfare programs in the years since.

All the women referenced in the novel who reside outside of Horton were real people who participated in the Women's Suffrage movement. A simple Wikipedia search will reveal 21 pages of history including an excellent bibliography with dates and events in the United States.

I begin the novel with several stanzas of the poem, "Lincoln, A Man of the People," by Edwin Markham, poet laureate of Oregon in 1929. Abraham Lincoln's image was placed on the five-dollar bill in 1915 and his monument is pictured on the back of the bill (the only president so honored). In the 1920s he had become more popular than George Washington. He had risen from the status of "common man" to that of President of the United States, and his hardships made identifying with him easier for many citizens. Markham's vision of Lincoln was a template for the modern man of the 1920s. Later stanzas of the second poem by Markham begin chapter 12, "The Man With the Hoe." This other of Markham's important works simply asks the question: How much of who we are as individuals of grace is lost when we labor like the ox, because we have to survive. Sketches were placed at the front of nearly every chapter by design, in the hopes of stimulating the imagination of thoughtful readers who often just need to be reminded to put their electronic devices down and contemplate the world around them. Feel free to color the sketches your way.

David Hascall

ACKNOWLEDGEMENTS

Philip Chancey, who agreed to provide sketches for this work succumbing to bribes of pizza and muffins.

Sandra Craven, who found time to proofread the manuscript in the midst of working full time and planning three weddings. Your encouragement was pure gold!

Barbara Gleason, owner of CraneDance Publications, who with gentle encouragement brought the manuscript to life.

Barbara Hascall, the Laurie in my life, who graded papers and made countless batches of soap in our kitchen while I wrote. And, who took control during a difficult time in my life, and assured me with one sentence, "It's not going to be this way."

Kathleen Hascall, my mother, who played with tin plates and knew Billy Whiskers. And, who nursed me through the injuries endured by Grayson Palmer and Hiram Jack in this book.

Earl Kelley, for tagging me with, "I've been waiting for someone to pick this story up and you're it." And, "I thought you were going to make a movie out of the story."

Jeff Moses, who agreed to edit this work in the midst of training for a half-marathon, and starting a new job, without giving it a second thought.

Marlie Moses, Jeff's mother, who offered additional editing gems and who insisted I refine my writing style in the midst of her own writing commitments and health challenges.

Sanford David Rice, owner of the Horton Store for more than 40 years, who made me swear an oath to return precious pictures and documents of the history of Horton, Oregon. As the local historian, your assistance was invaluable.

William T. Vollmann, who let me help him do research on one of his books, and prompted countless re-writes of this manuscript with one simple rule: Follow where the research leads. Shoot straight, Bill.

Richard Winston, who asked me to help him locate the Horton Railroad grade in 1972, while working on his master's degree at the University of Oregon. Raised in the woods, it was an easy find for me.

Bob Stroda of Monroe, Oregon, who let me photograph the log car likely used on the Horton Railroad. A picture can be found in the appendix.

Gloria Zirges, creator of the quilt shown at a necessary but unfortunately small size on the cover, which was awarded best in show at the annual Newport, Oregon, Quilt festival in 2012. The quilt is a tribute to Gloria's grandmother who lived in a sod house.

Gregg Scott, photographer of the quilt that was created by Gloria Zirges.

Ernie Smyth, of High Pass, who I interviewed in 2005 at the Bear Creek end of the grade. How could I forget the wild ride along the old railroad grade in a Gator?

Ray Wolfe of Horton, Oregon, whom I also interviewed in 2005 at the Horton end of the grade. Born and raised in the Horton Valley, his dad helped build the Horton railroad. At 84, Ray talked about his own road-building career with a diesel-powered cat; he was still operating a one-man sawmill in 2005, though I declined the invitation to watch him work it.

The Sisters of Good Shepherd Orphanage in Guanajuato, Mexico, who pray for me and my mother every day. These gracious elderly women, themselves vanishing, taught me that children come and go, but their voices sometimes never leave the orphanage. A portion of the proceeds for this book will go to provide continuing support for the orphanage. A picture of one of the Sisters and some of the children can be found in the appendix.

Special thanks to authors Joe Blakeley, Mycheille Norvell, and Tom Titus for also reviewing the manuscript and offering valuable insights.

David Hascall   The Longest Wooden Railroad

PROLOGUE

"It's taking too long," *Hiram said out loud. Any second now, Hiram Jack, grade master of the new railroad shortcut, expected the eerie quiet that surrounded him to be shattered by exploding dynamite. Despite the fog that blanketed the valley below, obstructing his view of the explosions, he had heard the other three clearly and was sure of the count: BOOM! BOOM! BOOM!*

But, one of the charges, the one closest to him, had not detonated. He had several final measurements to make at High Pass Crevice and debated whether he should do that first before investigating the unexploded charge. While he waited and paced, trying to make up his mind, thoughts of his wife Polly and their girls came to mind. They would be waiting for him, and the other families in Horton would be waiting likewise for their fathers and husbands to return from the workweek away as well. Friday nights were always a celebration when the crews got back to town.

The railroad crews were always anxious to head back to the bunkhouse early on Fridays to collect their belongings, then to travel back down the tracks to home in Horton. They had asked him to blow all the charges at the same time and be done with it. The men were eager to leave for home and the explosions would signal a celebratory cheer, especially on a Friday when work was over for the week.

He strained his ears, looking and listening to the West, toward the Lake Creek Valley. He wondered if he had miscounted. It had been a long week, good progress had been made and he was exhausted.

Hiram had decided to watch the explosions from his vantage point near High Pass Crevice, do some final measurements then hurry back to ride the new locomotive home.

The night before he had told Bull Kelly, the crew boss and rail superintendent, that he had other work to do up this way. Clearing the tree stumps out of the final stretch of the railroad right-of-way would show the progress that had been demanded of the crew and Hiram had decided to continue blasting all morning.

His decision to investigate the fourth charge planted under a large Douglas fir stump was a fateful one. When he approached through the fog he was nearly on top of the stump before he could see a thin ribbon of dirty blue smoke coming from the dynamite fuse. He turned and ran. The fourth explosion sent him flying like chaff in the wind. When he opened his eyes, though dazed, he was helped to his feet by Bull Kelly. When Bull spoke, Hiram could not hear his words and soon found himself being led back up hill to High Pass Crevice.

TABLE of CONTENTS

CHAPTER 1

A RIVER ON GLASS

LINCOLN, THE MAN OF THE PEOPLE

—Edwin Markham, 1852–1940

. . .

The color of the ground was in him, the red earth;
The smack and tang of elemental things:
The rectitude and patience of the cliff;
The good-will of the rain that loves all leaves;

. . .

Sprung from the West,
The strength of virgin forests braced his mind,
The hush of spacious prairies stilled his soul.
Up from log cabin to the Capitol,
One fire was on his spirit, one resolve:—
To send the keen axe to the root of wrong,
Clearing a free way for the feet of God.
And evermore he burned to do his deed
With the fine stroke and gesture of a king:
He built the rail-pile as he built the State,
Pouring his splendid strength
through every blow;
The conscience of him testing every stroke,
To make his deed the measure of a man.

. . .

Friday, March 1, 1929

Polly Jack sat alertly gazing out the living room window of the small company-owned house she shared with her husband and two daughters, hoping to catch a glimpse of a rare sunset through the gloomy gray of winter in the Oregon Coast Range. Looking East up toward High Pass, Polly had been drawn to the window an hour ago, unsure why. Normally she would gaze to the West. The shadows of growing darkness started first in the deepest canyons and valleys, swallowing the daylight with cold indifference, and then descended toward the Horton Mill. Some of the houses in town were already well lit, their kerosene lamps sparkling in anticipation of the coming evening. She watched the familiar progression of nightfall, feeling it press in toward her. She raised the wick on the hurricane lamp perched on the windowsill. Everyone would be gathering soon at the Horton general store, with the weekly return of the railroad crews.

Horton was an isolated lumber town with roads that were often impassable in winter. The eighteen-mile railroad being built through the Oregon Coast Range to the Southern Pacific tracks near Cheshire, Oregon, would bring new life to the entire Lake Creek Valley. Despite numerous ranches throughout the valley, logging and lumber were what mattered in Horton. The lumber mill was here and the railroad to carry the lumber out was being built here. It was all anyone talked about.

It would be the high point of the construction season if the tracks to the top of the railroad grade could be finished this month, Polly thought. The crews had accomplished so much; no one wanted to quit, even though the winter weather had been their constant enemy.

The last stretch of the construction, to High Pass Crevice, was the steepest part of the grade and the most dangerous. Instead of building around many of the large boulders and tree stumps, the crew now was blasting them aside with dynamite. Polly shifted uneasily in her chair: her husband, Hiram, would be directing the blasting, close to its destructive power.

She barely noticed a rivulet of water that ran down the outside of the windowpane. It followed a tortuous path, chasing the drops that had preceded it. Changing direction, the drips caught her eye. Polly stared at them thoughtfully. Her weathered face showed a mix of fatique with a hint of puzzlement and unsettled fear, as she sighed deeply. A wisp of hair fell across her forehead as she traced the water's anticipated pathway downward with her finger. The window glass was cold to the touch. A drop began to pick up speed for no apparent reason. As she watched, Polly wished it would defy its downward destiny. The droplet changed its course again as she watched, at last stopping at the bottom of the pane. Countless drops would merge along the ledge of the pane then flow sideways, finally falling onto the rock foundation. From here the fragile stream would soak into the soil and disappear.

Water always finds its way somewhere, she thought. She considered the drop of water she watched, following its downward path in her mind. Her chosen drops would flow underground down the hillside to Swartz Creek, then into Lake Creek, and finally into the Siuslaw River. Water from the valley flowed to the Pacific Ocean at Florence. She wondered how long the trip would take.

"Another day of countless indifferent drops," she said. "Is my life like this? Is my life like a river on glass, cold and without depth?"

She looked away from the window, closing her eyes. Lost in her thoughts, she began to reflect on her life in Horton since arriving three years ago. It was so different here than Ohio, she realized, shaking her head slowly. There were so few women in Horton. The rain and cold made it difficult to visit others. Polly thought of her many friends in the quilting circle back home. No one here had a house big enough for a quilting frame, she had discovered, and she reluctantly had given up the idea of a quilting circle. At times, the isolation she felt was almost unbearable. Speaking softly to herself, Polly whispered, "Husband, I can chase your dream only a little while longer, if I must."

The relentless rain soaked everything here, Polly reflected. She had gotten used to their clothes never quite drying during the winter months. Hiram never seemed to mind the soaking rain, and never complained. She admired his toughness, yet wished for something more from him. Will you ever understand how difficult being separated from my family and friends is for me, she wondered silently? Do you know how hard it is for the girls and me to be separated from you for five days every week? Suddenly, her pent up thoughts emerged, surprising her. "At times this house is no more than a prison," she said aloud, angrily.

Polly began thinking about the needs of her family. It always gave her focus at times of discontentment. She regularly offered to get Hiram some new water-resistant work clothes at the Horton General Store. His reply was always the same. At last, tired of her urging, he had told her flippantly, "You use what you have and wear it out, you make do, or do without."

Hiram had so few clothes. Polly had told him that if he wouldn't buy new clothes now and then, she wouldn't either. He never seemed to see her point. Even though they had a little money now, there was never quite enough for each of them to have something new. Extra money went for the girls. It was easiest that way.

Taking care of Hiram's clothes had become her top priority on weekends. She would turn the steaming denim over and over on their wood stove and flat irons in the evening, while the girls did their school work or read their favorite books. She knew every one of his shirts and socks, having turned them countless times to avoid scorching. They would be wet again soon enough from his sweat or from the rain. She could do this for the grade master of the new railroad. She would send him up the grade clean and dry on Monday mornings. "I am so proud of you," she whispered.

The rain in Oregon was better than the heat on their farm in Ohio, though. The awful humidity there, the failed crops, and the necessary chores every day were exhausting; it took the best out of them to get through each day.

It was so much easier here, she thought, in some ways. The girls were healthier here, even though the nearest doctor was in Junction City, a day or more away.

Polly began shaking her head slowly, a sly smile creeping across her face. "Hiram, my love," she said out loud. "You just weren't meant to be a farmer."

Now they were settled. They had a house, and the girls were happy even though they shared a bed and a bedroom. As long as their dry wood held out each winter they would be warm amidst the endless wet, foggy, grayness that she felt closing in on her at times.

This third winter seemed to last for an eternity. Polly had escaped at times, involving herself with the school board. She felt pride in the new school bus and the excellent teacher who had been hired from back in New York. Polly had been shocked after they arrived to see students during the winter months arrive for school from the southern end of the valley in the back of a wagon, covered only by a tarp. Polly told Hiram she had to try to help out. He expressed support for her involvement in the projects with the school, yet it had brought her only a temporary distraction from her longings for her Ohio friends and family. It had not interested Hiram in the end and her efforts to include him had not brought them closer together.

Polly knew she should feel more contented. Most days it was enough to be warm and dry. Tonight perhaps, there would be news that the crews had reached the summit. If not, maybe it would happen next week. Polly's mind began to drift again. She was restless tonight but unsure why. Perhaps it was the blasting along the grade on Fridays, she reasoned. From ten miles away the echoes of the blasting off the hillsides around Horton were a reminder of the confinement that she could not escape. The constant noise was also a deadly reminder that her husband's work was serious business.

Suddenly dark thoughts, like a cloud before a thunderstorm, rolled over her. Sadness overwhelmed her. Polly began thinking of her father's sudden death. She fought to send the sadness away, replacing it with good memories. She and Hiram had met at her father's funeral. It was an odd beginning for their courtship. Hired to fill the grave, Hiram looked so out of place that day, watching the grieving family for a sign to begin his grim task. Polly watched tears form in Hiram's eyes that day across the tight family circle around her father's coffin. She found comfort in this stranger's tears. She was moved to discover more about him, and felt he must be a kind man.

Times had been hard from the beginning. They seemed to be so unlucky. Despite financial help from both their families, crop failure after crop failure had taken everything. Hiram had become discouraged, so Polly renewed her efforts to make the farm successful. She remembered how hard she and their two young daughters, Tara and Rosie, had worked back then. Hiram was lost to her at times, dreaming of a fresh start out West. She had objected with all the tears she could muster with each plan he devised to leave Ohio.

Without her knowledge, Hiram had responded to a newspaper ad for the position of grade master for a rail line being built in the Oregon Coast Range. When the letter came from the Horton Railroad on official-looking stationery, he became impossible to live with. He could talk of nothing else. He would purchase a Model T Ford Runabout Pickup, trading the little equity they had left in their farm. Polly and the girls would move in with her Aunt Gladys. Hiram would send money when it was time for them to join him. After a flurry of arrangements, he left for Oregon within a week.

Alone and resentful, Polly had been unsure about the future of her marriage. After his letter arrived, it took her a week to decide to follow Hiram. It was the hardest decision she had ever made. She finally decided to follow him, committing to the isolation of the Oregon woods and trusting him to have all of their best interests in his heart. Did he have room for all of them along with his dreams? So far, their life together seemed to be a failure in the areas that mattered most to her: feeling an equal partnership. Friends had suggested that Oregon and a fresh start might be her only chance at keeping the family together. A secure job with a steady income was surely what they needed most. Reluctantly, she accepted the advice of her quilting group.

Polly was suddenly alert. She knew that Hiram would be hungry tonight…for more than just food. Raising her eyebrows with a sly smile, she understood what he needed most from her. Five days apart every week gave them little time for being a family or for lovemaking. She smoothed her straight brown hair back from her face, beginning to prepare her mind and body for him. I can make his favorite dessert tonight, apple dumplings, she thought. "Someday, we will look back on all this," she uttered.

Lost for words to describe her conflicted feelings, Polly frowned. It occurred to her at that moment that she spent much of her free time reaching back into the past for comfort today. There had been so little reward here, she reasoned, except for the joy the children brought to both of them. There is always comfort in the girls, she remembered. Still, Polly knew that she must look beyond Horton.

She gave in, letting her mind drift back in time to unanswered questions about the Horton Railroad project. No one seemed to know or care how long the work would last. All estimates she heard for completion had been inaccurate. How could building a railroad through the mountains be completed in three months? Polly began searching for an answer. Finally, the words came to her.

"Dreamers," she said out loud. They were all dreamers, she recounted, starting with that scoundrel Joseph Arnold. In the beginning, he had peddled his ideas door to door, the neighbors said, then left with their money. "You're all still dreaming," Polly said, speaking to no one in particular.

She shook her head slowly. Smiling, she remembered Hiram's recent words, when asked about the wooden tracks to support the heavy locomotive and railroad cars. "Money to support the project keeps coming in, Polly, my love, we can't quit now," he had said. "When it wears out in a spot we just replace it. Raw material is all around us."

"It wobbles here and there, but we're used to that," Polly said, mimicking her husband's voice.

Polly stood, and walked into the corner of their living room. She removed the blanket carefully and gazed at Hiram's masterpiece: the scale model bridge and trestle designed to span High Pass Crevice. He had completed it only the previous month. Now, after the model's return from Junction City, it had a permanent place in the corner. Bull Kelley, who had been appointed the superintendent of the railroad project, had approved of the model and shared the design with the governing board and a group of potential investors in Junction City. Hiram had received a small pay raise for getting the model completed in time for the investors' meeting. Polly had heard that photos of the bridge had appeared in the Junction City Times. Reporters from the Eugene and Portland newspapers had also expressed interest.

The combined company, formed by the three Horton brothers, owners of the lumber mill, and inventor Joseph Arnold, had created the Arnold, Junction City & Horton Railroad project. The requirement that part of Hiram's wages be taken in rail stock, a recent change for all employees, had confused them both. However, the company had convinced them they were becoming owners. They would share in the profits, when lumber arrived in the Willamette Valley. Their stock certificates did spend like cash, she had discovered, in Junction City and at the nearby Horton General Store.

Polly knew what their evening would be like. They would hurry through dinner, put the girls to bed, and wait for them to fall asleep. As they undressed, Hiram would share the week's progress, including a revised estimate of the completion date of the project. They would make frantic love, then both would fall asleep exhausted.

Hiram was so thin now, she reflected, and tired. He often spent most of his weekends in bed, the girls playing nearby. They would build a blanket playhouse over chairs using the covers of their bed while he dozed. He seemed to rest peacefully when he could hear the sound of their voices in happy play.

The girls would sing his favorite song over and over again tonight, she knew, which always delighted Hiram. He would dance around the room with them while they sang:

> *"Hinky Dinky Parlay Voo.*
> *Many a son of Abraham,*
> *Ate his ham for Uncle Sam,*
> *Hinky Dinky Parlay Voo."*

Why this particular song delighted her husband, she did not know. There were things he had done in the war she knew so little about. Her only clues had been mumbled words in restless sleep, about mustard gas and trenches. His brief Army experience building trench defenses with wooden barricades and barbed wire in France was his only engineering experience. It had been enough however, to land the grade master job that came with a cramped company house.

CHAPTER 2

PROSELYTIZE OR PERISH

Four Billion board feet! With lumber at seven and eight dollars a thousand, the Horton mill easily sawed 50,000 board feet per day. If a mill owner could generate a dollar a thousand profit over and above expenses…that was a lot of money in those days.

—Earl Kelley, in *No Way to ~~Run~~ / Build a Railroad*

B ull Kelly, railroad superintendent, had been called to Junction City to a special company board meeting before the Gentry's first run up the grade. He had made the long trip by car, bumping over the twisty and deeply rutted Mapleton-Junction City Highway, swearing at the inconvenient timing, and thinking of ways to keep his job. He fumed as he waited for the water level to drop at the floating log bridge over Lake Creek, at the junction of Horton Road and Mapleton-Junction City Highway. He had been stuck there for several hours, waiting for the bridge to realign with the road so that he could cross.

"For God's sake, what's the rush?" he muttered to himself. Recent rainfall always held up traffic leaving Horton, isolating the community. Watching a horse-drawn wagon going by on the other side of the bridge added to his annoyance.

While he waited, he wondered why the railroad board chose to meet in a feed store. It is still too soon to know if the "loco" they bought can pull a load of logs over the grade, he thought to himself. They were up to something, that's for sure. He examined his letter of invitation, but it gave him no clue. An uneasy feeling deep in his sizable frame made him squirm in the seat and drum his fingers on the dashboard of the new company car. The Chrysler Imperial E-80 bought for the Horton brothers was a car for showing money, Bull considered, a knowing smile spreading over his face. While waiting, he thumbed through the "new car manual," noticing the vehicle had a top speed of 80 miles an hour.

"Of course," he muttered. "E-80 for 80 miles an hour top speed, but not on this road."

Looking around the inside of the four-door touring car, he pushed down on the passenger seat, testing the cushion forcefully. It was nice inside he had to admit. Too nice for that bunch, he thought. He found the registration card in the visor and saw the Chrysler was registered in the names of all three of the Horton Brother, owners of the Horton saw mill. Those three do-gooders plan to get rich with my railroad, he thought, his mood continuing to sour. They own the mill but they don't own me. I wonder how much stock those three own? They're in deep, I know it, he mused. Maybe they called the board meeting. Bull could not remember any confrontation between any of his crew and the mill workers recently. Nodding his head, an idea came to him.

"Getting nervous, boys?" Bull questioned aloud. "Running out of money?"

"Always for the show," he said thoughtfully, thinking about what he would say in his report. He looked around the spacious interior of the car a second time. His eyes fell upon the model of the bridge that grade master, Hiram Jack, had made. It was secure on the back seat, an odd but stout-looking bridge model with cables holding up the wooden span. At least I have this to show them, he thought.

He began rehearsing and practicing one of his unique skills. He worked the chaw in his mouth and marked the distance to a nearby bush. His first attempt was a direct hit. It was a sign. He suddenly felt powerful and knew how he would handle them. He would have to explain away the construction delays. The project was now more than four years behind schedule. He would use old and reliable arguments one more time and hope his aim was good.

The assembled board members and guests all glared at him when he entered the makeshift boardroom, a hastily converted storage room at the back of the Junction City Feed and Seed Store. There was something about their solemn nods of recognition that was unsettling. Success today might hinge on the smallest detail of his performance. He gave them his rehearsed smile of confidence, waving at some, shaking hands with others, as if they were old friends. He cleared his throat and spit an enormous chaw defiantly into a nearby spittoon; hitting it perfectly. It's my show now, he thought to himself.

He began his prepared speech, hoping to help them recall the progress he had achieved in reaching High Pass Crevice, as reported at the previous meeting. He was giving his best performance, "We have a solution now to the sinking grade problem and I brought you the design for the High Pass Trestle Bridge." Slowly unveiling the bridge model, he could hear chairs moving as the investors stood to get a closer look.

"The bridge across the crevice is the last major hurdle I see," he said. "We have a little blasting and grade work next week and we hope to build the bridge soon after. We should be able to connect the tracks within a month."

"The line will be complete from Horton all the way to the top, gentlemen. The track is stout," Bull boasted. "The wooden tracks need regular repair, as you know. There is no rock under it for ballast, remember. The trestle pilings eventually give out under the weight of the train, but are easier to replace than whole sections of sunken grade."

"My crews are working full speed despite being short-handed and the need to deal with the tough weather," Bull added. "We are dropping the last of the timber in our path directly on the rail bed, packing it down ahead of the rails. We will be done before you know it, if your Bear Creek crews do their part. Of course, if we all had rock to raise the bed we could have kept to the original schedule and avoided that muddy mess along Swartz Creek."

Bull stopped speaking and glanced around the room, looking for any sign of enthusiasm in the crowd. He knew he didn't need to say more on the subject of the lack of crushed rock for ballast under the rails.

It was always his ace to play when they complained too hard about the cost overruns and delays in completing the project. He was right and they all knew it. "Rock is too expensive and unavailable," he had been told countless times. "Use what is available on site." To the grade builders that meant using wood for everything including strengthening the ballast under the rails to keep a smooth incline to the grade.

Bull cautiously continued, suddenly feeling defensive again. "I'm here to tell you, my men work their hearts out for this company. I'm getting the best out of 'em, but we are still short handed. My boys think this track building is a race to the top of the grade to High Pass Crevice. It is a matter of pride for them to beat the East-side crews. I did tell them there might be a bonus in it."

A murmur of disagreement arose from the crowd. Bull raised his hand, gesturing for quiet. "But if there is not enough money for that, then we'll give them more stock, just like before." Bull caught himself again looking around the room for some sign of reassurance. Not seeing any, he began to wonder what had happened. "There is no money bonus of course," he said, speaking slowly and deliberately, "without your permission." He suspected a rumor had reached the board about a promised bonus. Maybe the Horton Brothers ratted on me, he thought. Is that what this is all about? Was this what had cooled the reception to his enthusiastic presentation, or was it something else?

Bull Kelly wanted to keep his job. It had been a stroke of genius, he told himself, to bring the bridge model. He was becoming unsettled, however, by the continued quiet in the room. He pressed on, with several other things on his mind.

"Winter is a difficult time in the high country," Bull continued. His dramatic gesturing toward the thin white line of snow that had conveniently fallen the night before in the coast range, caused eyes to move toward the windows in the improvised boardroom. Bull sensed he was making progress.

"Lastly," he began, holding up the local newspaper. "I know I don't have to remind you that the Horton-Junction City railroad shortcut is very popular with the local newspapers. Here is another article in the paper about your brilliant plan to open up an area to logging that has not been touched. It says here, 'There is a lifetime of timber up there.' Bull raised a newspaper up for the crowd to see. "Your investment will put both Junction City and the whole Lake Creek Valley on the map. That's why my crews are working their hardest to finish the line in the dead of winter. Everyone in the valley is behind this thing."

Walking across in front of the packed room, he began to survey the stern faces. Purposely making eye contact with each man in the front row, Bull looked desperately for hopeful sign. Thinking frantically, he remembered another important point he wanted to make. "Think of the jobs you're making," Bull said, increasing his volume as he spoke. "We have the timber cruising estimate now. I checked the figures myself. There is four billion board feet of timber in the Lake Creek Valley. It will soon be yours, once we complete the last stretch and link to Bear Creek. Then, all you need is a short spur to the track coming from Alvadore to be connected to the whole Southern Pacific rail system, Eugene to the South, and Portland to the North. The logs are almost falling onto the train now," Bull mused. There was soft laughter from the group. He had them at last!

"You do your part and keep the investors coming." Bull continued, his voice trailing off. Suddenly, he sensed that he had just struck a nerve and said the wrong thing. "There is too much at stake for us to stop now," he interjected, trying to recover. "Take care of the men and their families when they come to town, here," Bull added. "My rail building crew will be your timber falling crew next year. We got work here and profits for the next fifty years!" The room at last offered him a guarded applause.

The room quickly went silent again. There were no questions, and an awkward silence followed. Finally, a lone investor dressed in a top hat stood up and demanded a tour of the rail line from the west side.

Anxious now to please, Bull replied that he would set it up as soon as the weather broke. "We're blasting the last of it this week, above the Hole, near the Crevice. I only let a few powder monkeys up there, so give me a little more time to tidy up. "Dynamite makes a mess!" he said loudly, smiling through brown-stained teeth.

Bull began moving toward the door offering a dismissive wave. "I got to get back to my crews if there are no more questions. You got the terminus there at Bear Creek finished for the show, right?" No one in the audience responded. "Just remember not to take folks too far along up there —not much track in places 'till we can get you the rail lumber from the Horton mill. When we break over the top, you'll know. You should hear us blasting along the 'hog back,' I mean the ridge, next week," Bull concluded, his voice trailing off. He quickened his pace toward the exit.

The Board Chairman got up and made an announcement that froze Bull in his tracks. "Gentleman, the next item on the agenda: the summary of the stock offering results from the demonstration of the log unloading station at Bear Creek is cancelled." Bull knew the event had been hastily planned but he did not know it had already occurred and failed to impress new investors. Later he would learn that the steam donkey hoist engine failed to reach pressure. The track, visible from the station, had washed out from recent flooding and made for some embarrassing questions. As a result not a single new investor had stepped forward, and not a single stock certificate had been sold. The event had been a disaster.

Bull was anxious to get away from the meeting. Breathing a heavy sigh, he climbed back into the company car, anxious to reward himself with a chaw and a drink. A carefully concealed quart jar labeled, "Singing Black Top," was in his hand as he neared the junction of Ferguson Road and Territorial Highway. He guzzled the pale liquid eagerly, toasting his success at keeping his job, enjoying the burning in his throat. He had brought his private stock of first skimming moonshine from Horton, from the still belonging to his friend Coal, the tender for the burner at the

Horton Mill. Breaking the rules always made the liquor taste even better.

When Bull drove by the log dumping station at Bear Creek, six miles from Junction City, he could tell the Bear Creek side of the project was in trouble. It was clear by the mess he observed that money was being wasted. Tools were lying around the work site, gates and doors were open and no watchman was on duty. In a moment of unusual loyalty, Bull drove back to Junction City and went to the only telephone in town. His first call was to Portland. Joseph Arnold, the major stockholder in the railroad, needed to know about the Bear Creek disaster. Bull had not seen him at the meeting and doubted if anyone had the courage to tell him that the east side of the project was in such poor shape. He would of course offer his services to get the Bear Creek crews back on schedule.

He was told that Mr. Arnold was not in and was instructed by Mr. Arnold's secretary to make a call to the Eugene Hotel. Bull knew that the upscale Eugene Hotel, was the only place Mr. Arnold's right hand man Willard Spencer would stay.

CHAPTER 3

THE GENTRY

David Hascall   The Longest Wooden Railroad

Witnesses recall delivery of this new locomotive in 1929. It was hauled over Low Pass to the mill in Horton by truck and trailer.

–Earl Kelley, from *No Way to ~~Run~~ / Build a Railroad*

Friday Evening, March 1, 1929

Fourteen year-old Grayson Eliot Palmer, his first name shortened to Gray by his grandfather, jumped up and down impatiently on the wooden tracks, eager to catch a glimpse of the arriving train over the heads of anxious families in front of him. At the height of each jump the laminated planks that made up the wooden tracks were visible all the way to the edge of Horton. He was hoping to be the first to spot the train's new locomotive. Most Horton families were there or soon would be, and they all knew the train was close when they heard an exchange of whistles between the train's engine and the sawmill.

The new-style locomotive, described as a "Geared Steam Logger," was making its first run home down the grade today, and the event had created a festive atmosphere. The people of Horton believed their future rested on the success of this odd-looking custom-built iron horse. Built close-by in Portland, it had seventeen forward gears, one reverse gear and hard rubber wheels grooved on the outside edge to ride on the inside of the wooden rails.

Thus far, the engine had performed well, reaching twelve miles an hour as reported by the train crew. However, its major challenge lay ahead, with the completion of the steepest section of the incline. Transporting lumber for construction of the rails and trestles up the grade and over High Pass, then down the east slope to Bear Creek, was necessary to complete the project. The new train would need to pull lumber cars stacked high with freshly cut planks, each one measuring two inches by eight inches and sixteen feet long, up an eight percent grade, then across grade master, Hiram Jack's trestle bridge. The grade then descended to Bear Creek near the Territorial Highway outside of Junction City.

Gray's grandfather Verin Palmer had nicknamed the new engine, "The Gentry," after a local celebrity—a hard-working mule. Mr. Gentry was the lead mule that pulled the steam donkey in the early days of constructing the rail line and he was remembered with fondness by the local townspeople. Fondly, that is, except by Bull Kelly, the superintendent and self-appointed train engineer, who strongly objected to the naming of the engine for the donkey.

"This here is my locomotive and I'm no gentry!" Bull barked the words at Gray as the train left the Horton store on Monday. "You tell old Verin that for me," he bellowed, an enormous chaw of tobacco firmly embedded between his front lip and teeth.

Verin had sympathized with the retired "forgotten mule," as he described his feelings for Mr. Gentry to Gray. His care had extended to exercising Mr. Gentry daily with walks along the grade. When Mr. Gentry passed away, Verin retreated to his rocking chair, lost interest in playing cribbage with Gray and stopped eating. Gray was beside himself seeing his grandfather so unhappy.

"Leave me be. I'm seventy-three years old and I can sit here all day long if I choose," his grandfather barked at him one day. "My bones are tired."

When Gray mentioned the new iron horse needed a name, his Grandfather seemed to rally, believing that his old walking companion needed to be remembered. Soon Verin had convinced the Horton brothers, part owners in the locomotive, and many of the rail workers who frequented Molly's boarding house, to honor the mule in this way.

Gray had a good idea why he had attracted attention from Bull. He had stowed aboard the old truck engine used to pull the lumber cars weeks before, and had ridden all the way to the first big turn in the grade called Big Bend. He had been able to remain hidden until the line of cars emerged from the Swartz Creek tunnel, some six miles from Horton. The grade leveling crew, known to all as gandy dancers, had laughed at Bull for giving "free rides," and Bull had not forgotten that embarrassment. Nevertheless, Bull had many reasons for keeping snooping eyes away from the rail grade.

After a hard week of building the railroad grade using hand tools, the Horton crews were, as always, anxious to get home for the weekend. Working from the west end of the railroad grade had been much harder than projected for the crew of thirty men who had started the project. Now the number of men had shrunk to a mere twenty. Workers seemed to quit at random, citing weather problems or illness. Oddly, there were very few injuries reported.

The winter rains stopped progress altogether some days, when seas of mud buried the grade work of previous days. The crews fought back with their picks and shovels, clearing and rebuilding the path for the Gentry. Bull had gotten them to do the most hazardous work on Friday mornings, knowing they would agree to anything as long as their work ended early that day. Injuries, although rare, generally happened on Friday. Without a doctor within fifty miles, an injured man would have to wait until the whole crew could be assembled to return to Horton.

At Friday noon, work was over for the week. The crew was ready for warm fires, dry clothes and their families. The hastily constructed bunkhouse ten miles up the grade, made of rough-cut lumber, gave the crew a chance to clean up and pack their wash for the weekend. Bull knew how to get the most out of the men. The crew joked that they were getting something for nothing and that felt good. Bull's mention of a bonus for the fastest crew to the top, between the east and west side, kept the men working hard as well. It's just as well that the A, JC &

H Auto Rail Company Board of Directors would never know they paid for a full day of work on Friday; they didn't usually get it.

The wide crevice at High Pass required a major engineering feat, and for that Hiram Jack had been hired. Those who ventured as far as the top shook their head at what he would have to design. The steepest part of the grade led up to the crevice and there seemed no way to maintain a steady six-percent grade, a standard for a loaded train pulling uphill. Hiram's goal of eight percent was unthinkable on iron rails. But, no one knew if wooden tracks were any better or worse. Slippage on the rails meant disaster—a quick trip back down the grade—and a likely derailment. Hiram planned to gradually add weight to the Gentry's cars going up hill until the train began to slip. To stop the tracks from sinking in the mud or washing out, he began raising the grade with wooden poles made into trestles almost along the entire length of the west side of the grade.

The move had finally reduced the steepest incline to eight percent at the top. However, it increased the cost of the whole line by $5000 per mile. Bull Kelly had reluctantly agreed with each design change, and the predictable construction delay. The test would come when the Gentry pulled the first load up and over the trestle bridge.

The span across High Pass Crevice would be a blend of Hiram's well-tested trestle system and a cable suspension bridge. Hiram had decided it would have to be built from the Horton side. His final bridge design had been incomplete until recently and he had been accused of wasting time. Bull had lost patience explaining the increased cost to the board and investors. Everyone knew you didn't cross Bull Kelly.

The small wage concession on Fridays had endeared Bull to the crew, and he always added to the unwritten bonus by improving his best time each week getting back down the grade to Horton. Curves and trestles seemed to be the sturdiest designs all the way down, Bull had to admit. However, trestle repairs were constant, requiring part of his crew every week.

If the crew was riding the train home and the trestle began to shake badly when the crew crossed over it, the spot would make the list for repair the following week. If a trestle had not received repair in a timely fashion, Bull would put the engine in gear, make the crew get off and let the engine pull the log cars across without anyone on board. The crew would run down the incline and up the other side, remount the lumber cars, and continue on down toward Horton.

A major investor—and prominent board member—was rumored to have taken over supervision of the East side work crew to speed things up. Sometimes called the "Lazy Bear Creek Bunch," they had what seemed to be the easiest grade to build, yet had just as many delays in construction as their Horton counterparts. Building in haste over flat grade, laying ballast on the ground without rock to stabilize and raise the rails had proved to be a poor engineering decision on both sides of the project.

When the Long Tom and Willamette rivers flooded and ran together in January of 1929, Bull insisted that the Horton crew be more sympathetic to their East side counterparts. Entire sections of flat-grade track had washed out, they were told, forcing a complete design change for that side of the project.

The practice of raising the grade with trestles eventually became standard practice on both sides, after several from the design crew shifted to the east side of the project with Hiram's designs. The race to the top was on.

However, there was still little both crews could do at times, except wait for the ground to dry out.

On weekends, while the Horton crew was at home with their families, many of the Bear Creek crew, working on the other end of the eighteen-mile shortcut railroad, could be found in Junction City, some six miles from their construction site. On occasion, their bunkhouse also flooded from winter rains, leaving minimal available housing, except for the city jail. When their money and credit ran out in Heiney's Speakeasy on Friday nights they would cause just enough trouble to get a jail invitation for the weekend.

...

How far did they get this week? Gray wondered. He knew that if he listened hard at the Horton General Store he would hear easily the best and worst of the news in the first five minutes after the crew returned. The questions were often the same.

"Anybody hurt today? How far beyond the Big Bend were they laying track? How far, now, to the High Pass Crevice? Anybody hear from the Bear Creek bunch this week?"

Normally, paychecks were distributed after the crew arrived and the crowds quickly dispersed. Horton families would scoop up their children and rush home, eagerly anticipating warmth, dry clothes and home-cooked meals. Tonight, however, there would be a speech about how the new engine had performed and hopefully important news of progress toward the summit of the grade. For Gray, the excitement was not to be missed.

CHAPTER 4

WHAT YOU HEAR CAN BE DECEIVING

Many of their accomplishments observed years later brought both marvel and admiration. How did they do it? They called it "common sense," or "horse sense." Years later, it was relegated by those not so impressed as "native intelligence.

−Earl Kelley, in *No Way to ~~Run~~ / Build a Railroad*

Friday Night, March 1, 1929

Someone spotted the steam plume from the locomotive's boiler exhaust and the parade atmosphere began. Like a band majorette, the Gentry led a musical procession of loaded log cars into Horton, coming to a stop at the Horton General Store. The watchman atop the Horton mill's four-story burner was the first to see it, the exhaust billowing skyward like scoops of cream-colored sherbet. A hand gesture to the mill foreman below resulted in a loud and melodious blast of warning from the mill's steam whistle that startled the waiting townspeople. The wooden tracks began to vibrate beneath Gray's feet, and people moved to either side of the rails, out of the way, opening a path for the train.

When the Gentry answered with its own high-pitched whistle, cheers erupted, hats waved and colorful scarves sliced through the evening sky in figure eights.

The sounds of the arriving train reached Horton as the last of the loaded log cars emerged from the Swartz Creek Tunnel, six miles away. The rail line's approach to Horton passed through a narrow canyon along the banks of Swartz Creek, and was flanked on both sides by giant old growth fir trees. Sounds magnified and changed as they funneled toward Horton. A continuous colliding echo rushing ahead of the train bounced back and forth across the hills above the town. The resulting "chop-flop, chop-flop" seemed to come from all directions.

Heads turned and people looked at each other with questioning looks, as the Gentry powered toward them.

Moving over flexing wooden rails, the rubber tires, iron wheels, and steam engine's orchestral sounds together added to the strange sonata. It was indeed a memorable entry. Later, many would describe the approaching train as the Gentry "two-step."

When the Gentry steamed past the first houses parallel to the main street in town, the cheers from the crowd grew louder. The cacophony of reverberating sound gave the whole train an air of mystery beyond its size. Someone in the crowd joked that a monster was emerging from the Horton woods. Joyous laughter rose from a town of wives, woodworkers, and wide-eyed children.

Hanging precariously off the log cars, arms waving to onlookers, the Horton "gandy dancers," trestle carpenters, and "powder monkeys" aboard the train made their entrance into Horton. As the train slowed, Bull Kelly again blew the steam whistle mounted above the Gentry's cab. More shouts of approval arose from the crowd.

As the Gentry rumbled past, Gray saw Bull Kelly at the controls. Suddenly, a giant wad of chewing tobacco landed on Gray, who could hear Bull laughing through his brown-stained teeth.

"Someday," Gray said angrily, wiping the nasty brown goo from his shirt, "I will drive the Gentry by myself. I'm going to pull that whistle cord for a full minute." Maybe, someday that Bull won't be around, Gray thought to himself. He let his angry notion pass in the carnival excitement of the train's arrival. Gray began running along side the train, his excitement returning.

"If it isn't the boy with the color name," Bull sneered at Gray, as he pushed forward the large lever brake that brought the train to a stop. Knowing the taunt was meant as an insult, Gray's pulse began to rise and his face flushed with color. He tried to fend off Bull's ridicule with a shrug of his shoulders and a sheepish grin to those around him.

There was a final ritual of shutting down the Gentry that distracted Bull, and Gray slipped into the crowd out of his sight. From the safety of the crowded street, Gray turned back toward the Gentry and began copying Bull's final movements inside the cab. He moved each knob and lever in the air, and checked the gauges just as Bull did. Anyone observing the act would have imagined Gray was a puppet on a string mirroring Bull's every movement. After the last step, the opening of the steam relief valve, the engine's idle ceased and Gray lost interest.

Hurrying along the tracks, Gray was intent; he was looking for the Indian head penny he had left on one rail before the train's arrival. A smashed penny from the Gentry's first trip down the grade would certainly be worth something, he was sure. The Indian head coin had come from the milk money jar in his Grandpa Verin's kitchen. He knew it was wrong to take it, but he hoped to trade it for something more valuable, something his Grandpa might even like.

Everyone Gray knew respected his grandfather. Verin Palmer had walked the Oregon Trail as a boy, all the way from St. Louis and over the Barlow Road. As the only remaining living pioneer in Horton, Verin was a local celebrity. Although the same stories of his Oregon Trail adventure were often repeated, no one seemed to mind. Everyone was needed in Horton. Verin Palmer's homespun wisdom was often in demand. "Horton is just a wagon train without wheels," he had told Gray. "We have to bring the world to us; that's what the railroad means."

David Hascall The Longest Wooden Railroad

CHAPTER 5

WORDS of COMFORT

David Hascall   The Longest Wooden Railroad

Isaiah Slayter purchased a German coach horse for $1,000. This imported animal was used by many valley residents to upgrade their stock. He was fed one egg per day to keep his coat shiny.

–Lane County Historian, Vol. XXXV, No. 2, Summer, 1990

Friday Evening, March 1, 1929

The Montgomery Ward mail-order catalog lay open on Rosie's nightstand. Rosie Jack, the younger daughter of Polly and Hiram Jack, had been turning the pages in her favorite catalog, which her friends called the "Wish Book." Curled, cut-out pages gave evidence that the seasonal catalog had been well-used. Rosie, now a teenager, enjoyed looking at pictures of women's clothing, and found the stylish fashions of women's underclothing, a specialty of the Montgomery Ward catalog, to be the most interesting. Rosie had the winter issue and could hardly wait until the spring catalog arrived.

The kerosene lamp in the bedroom she shared with her sister, Tara, burned brightly. Rosie's mother had recently trimmed the flat cotton wick of the lamp. It would be time for dinner soon, but Rosie wished she could have gone down the hill, to join the fun at the Horton General Store. When she heard the train whistle, she rushed to the window to watch the drama unfold—the arrival of the Gentry—in the fading light below. The cars, loaded with logs for the mill, would bring her father home. Everything seemed right when her father returned on Friday night.

Her mother had insisted Rosie help cook dinner tonight, a request she, of course, obeyed. Only when the Gentry's whistle blew a second time did she remember how much fun she had at the Horton Store on Friday nights. Tonight, though, it was Tara's turn to greet her father and bring him home.

Rosie enjoyed cutting out paper doll clothes from the catalog, mixing and matching outfits by the hour. She imagined how beauty queen Irene Ware might feel wearing the latest fashions from the catalog. "Do you have chores every day?" Rosie asked out loud, "Like I do?" She would show the best combinations of clothing she found that week to her father, cherishing his opinion above anyone else's. When she shared various clothing combinations with her sister Tara, her older sister would quickly lose interest. Men's riding jeans were the only clothes Tara ever cared about in the catalog.

The last book in the Billy Whiskers series, purchased from the catalog, lay open on her bedside dresser; the cloth bookmark Rosie had made drooped lazily from its pages. Rosie closed the book, returned it to the shelf and walked to the kitchen.

"Tara's down at the store, having all the fun," she whined. Her mother, Polly, ignored her. "Tara will greet father and hear all the news first," Rosie fumed to herself. Hiram and Tara would ride back up the hill doubling up on Scout, Tara's Welsh pony. Although the horse was small, only 14½ hands, he was a very strong pony.

Both Rosie and Tara had learned to ride on Scout. Their father had laughed at the pony a few times, teasing Tara that Scout was "just" tall enough to be considered a real horse. However, only Tara had kept up her riding, while Rosie, who preferred not to compete with her older sister, chose to do other things.

"Someday, Daddy will be proud of me, too, just like he is of Tara," Rosie said. Polly looked up from the pan of apple dumplings that were resting on the cast iron wood stove. Warm and fragrant, Polly drank in the aroma, while she thought. She gave Rosie a thoughtful glance. Polly put her arm around her youngest daughter, gave her a brief hug and the two of them walked to the window. They gazed into the growing darkness toward the Horton Store. Twinkling points of lights below allowed them to see that the Gentry had arrived. There was a crowd around the new locomotive.

"Maybe they're done with the blasting," Polly said encouragingly to Rosie. Rosie felt her mother's arm around her, but it was not enough to keep angry thoughts about her sister from overpowering her. She let them come, taking in a deep but ragged breath. Her mother's hug would make it safe to revisit them.

She had been cutting out paper dolls the previous day, when Tara leaped into their shared bedroom to report her terrible secret. She had learned how Rosie's name had been chosen. Tara began repeating over and over, "Your name is second-hand! You're second-hand Rosie, second-hand Rosie!

"Why is it second-hand, Tara? Tell me!" Rosie insisted. "I'll ask mother if you don't tell me," she warned Tara.

After a while, when it was clear that Rosie could no longer be held hostage by the game, Tara gleefully announced what she had learned. Tara's secret fell on Rosie like a giant fir. "Dad wanted a boy when you were born, and he had the name Roosevelt picked out, like the president. When you came out a girl he was so disappointed he couldn't think of any girls' names. So, mom just called you plain Rosie. You were supposed to be a boy, a boy, second hand Rosie, second hand Rosie, just like the song from the Follies," Tara sang taunting her younger sister.

"Stop!" Rosie shouted. "It's not true!" Rosie screamed, running from the room. Polly had been listening to her daughters from the kitchen. With Rosie clinging to her side, Polly gave a scolding look at Tara. "Why do you devil your sister so, Tara?"

Turning Rosie to face her, Polly spoke in a comforting tone. "What Tara told you is hurtful, but true. Your father and I both wanted boys to work the farm back in Ohio. Remember, all the work there was there? You carried water to the house in those big buckets, remember, Rosie?"

"I'm glad now the farm failed," Polly continued. "Your Papa wasn't cut out to be a farmer. He's a railroad man now and grade master suits him just fine. I couldn't run this house without both of you girls, Rosie," Polly said boldly, "I am glad you are a girl."

Tara bounced out of the room, triumphant in her hurtfulness. Rosie had begun to back away, shocked at what she had heard. "Come here, Rosie," her mother called to her. With Rosie encircled tightly in her arms, they were standing by the kitchen window, at the very moment Tara blazed by on Scout, riding at full gallop.

"When Tara was born it was the same with your father," Polly began. "He loves you both dearly, know that," Polly said. "He works hard for us, and don't you forget it." Polly continued, "You can see how your sister is, she still tries hard every day to give your father the son he wanted."

Tara made her second pass in front of the house on Scout, this time riding without holding onto the reins and waving her arms wildly.

"She is riding that horse right now straight up, wearing them jeans and acting just the way she thinks a man would act," Polly explained. "She doesn't think about it any more. Can't get your sister to wear a dress for anything. She'll never find a man acting the way she does." Polly said, slowly shaking her head. She hugged Rosie; then let her go.

Feeling that her daughter was still bothered by the revelation of the previous day, Polly spoke reassuringly. "I love how you're straight up about things Rosie. You're smart and I know you'll let this pass. Tara is a prisoner in them boys' clothes. I don't want to make the same mistake with you. What I have told you must never be repeated," her mother told her firmly. "Now you have a secret, too." Rosie's smile quickly returned.

"Fetch that pot holder there and take the dumplings off the stove, it's your father's favorite." Polly had abruptly changed the subject and ended their conversation about Tara. Rosie obeyed her mother eagerly; the apple dumplings, smothered in a pot holder, would soon be forgotten.

...

Gray began watching three of the other Horton kids, anxious to join their contest of pushing and shoving. The game was to see who could stand on the raised six-inch wide wooden rails the longest.

Tara arrived at the gathering at the Horton store, eager to join the fun. Seeing her school friends, most of whom were boys, she ran to join them. She understood the game the boys were playing instantly. Purposely running into the group, she sent them all sprawling to the ground. Tara landed on top of them, laughing with delight. "No one invited you, Tara," Gray said angrily.

"You seen my Pa yet," Tara asked?

"No, I have not seen your Pa," Gray barked back, speaking harshly.

Together the group turned and looked at the returning railroad men for Tara's father, grade master Hiram Jack. The other boys quickly lost interest and ran to the other side of the Gentry, leaving Tara and Gray.

Not finding her father with the group of men lined up for their weekly wages, Tara was immediately fearful. "He always rides in the first car," Tara said. "Gray, you look for him, too; help me find him!"

"Oh, all right," Gray, agreed reluctantly. While the townspeople listened to Bull's assessment of the week's work and the performance of the Gentry, the two continued walking through the assembled families looking for Hiram Jack.

Soon, Bull's assessment of the week's progress was fully reported and most importantly, the Gentry had performed as expected. Paychecks had been distributed and the crowd quickly thinned. Tara and Gray were left standing alone.

When the railroad superintendent began walking toward them, Tara immediately turned and fled. Gray turned and walked away. Tara heard the railroad man call after her. He was asking a question but she didn't want to hear it.

"Your Ma at home, girl?" Bull asked. "I don't see her here. I need to talk to her."

Tara couldn't answer. She knew something was wrong and it involved her father. She had to run. She needed to tell her mother that the railroad boss was coming. Running back to her pony, she leaped onto the startled animal's back and at the same time pointed him up the hill. Tara raced by the startled Bull Kelly so quickly it nearly knocked him to the ground. Bull watched her go streaking by, shook his head in surprise, and then trudged up the hill after her. His progress up the path to the Jack's hillside home was slowed by the growing darkness. Along the way he brushed off his company boiler suit with his grimy hands. He wanted to look presentable.

As he approached the house, Bull didn't know what he'd say, but things came to him when he was in a tight spot, just like at the board meetings—they always did. Tonight would be no different, he thought. He didn't need trouble with any of the crew or their families.

Despite the publicity disaster he had found at Bear Creek, Bull had no thoughts of leaving the railroad project, at least not yet. He would still have returned to Horton even if the board had fired him. What he had hidden in one of the dynamite shacks had to be kept a secret until the time was right, he had decided on the way back to Horton from Junction City. He knew he had crossed the line, with what he had done to Hiram Jack at High Pass Crevice. But, he told himself he simply had no choice. He would do whatever it took now, to keep his secret.

Tara came rushing through the front door, out of breath, having left Scout near the barn. Her mother rarely saw Tara with terror on her face. She knew something had happened.

"Papa wasn't on the train, Papa wasn't on the train," Tara repeated frantically, gasping to catch her breath. "That railroad man is coming here!" Tara reached wildly for her mother, tears pouring from her eyes.

"Slow down," Polly spoke reassuringly. "Tell me about Papa." Both girls began sobbing in unison. If Tara was crying, Rosie would cry, too. The girls looked into their mother's face for reassurance. They turned their heads in unison, startled as Bull Kelly cleared his throat. He was standing in their open doorway.

"Evening, Mrs. Jack," he said, clearing his throat again.

"Mr. Kelly," Polly replied cautiously. "What is the news, Mr. Kelly?"

"I'm afraid I have some bad news, Mrs. Jack. The crew told me your Hiram was surveying up near the Hole during the blasting this morning."

Tara sucked in an audible breath and begun to wail. Polly put her hand over Tara's mouth.

"They tell me they yelled for him to stay clear, but…" There was a pause in Bull's uncertain speech, heaving sobs now erupting from both the Jack girls. Bull raised a calming hand toward the girls, speaking in a reassuring voice. "We think he just missed the train, maybe dazed by the blasting, maybe he got lost. He's always in charge of the blasting you know. We leave him be to check things himself."

Polly began to crumble inside, but forced herself to focus on what Bull was telling her.

"You know we got a perfect record, I've never lost a man. I'll be leading a search party, myself, in the morning," Bull continued. "He may be just late for the train; we couldn't wait, you know, Friday night and all. He might be up at the bunk house, or walking down."

"It's too soon to worry, now, Mrs. Jack; let's all stay calm. I'm upset myself. I just come by to tell you; that's my job. Don't worry, he'll show."

Bull reversed his steps and quickly walked back to the mill. Smiling, he thought to himself, as he followed the darkened path downhill, "I'm a good one for a story."

Encircling both girls, Polly moved them to their bedroom. The three of them sat together on the girls' bed, holding each other. Polly let her girls sob, unable to offer reassurance, needing desperately to hold herself together. Stunned, a blank stare across her face, she fought the urge to panic. What did this mean, she wondered. My man always comes home. Finally, she began to softly sing and rock the girls.

> *When every earthly prop gives way,*
> *He then is my Hope and Stay.*
> *On Christ the Solid Rock, I Stand;*
> *All other ground is sinking sand.*

CHAPTER 6

THE SENTINELS

The world is changing fast. The roaring twenties were a heady time in history! Yes indeed, this was the time and the generation in all of history to accept such a challenge.

—Joseph Meeker, 1926

Friday Afternoon, March 1, 1929

Laurie Flanagan stood in the doorway of the schoolhouse watching the last of her students skip down the road toward the Horton General Store. Laurie drew in a deep breath, as she loosened the barrette that confined the single braid of long red hair. The coil quickly unraveled as Laurie shook her head gently from side to side. Laurie and Mildred Persons, the other teacher at the Horton School, had agreed upon a French bun style at the start of the school year. Neither of them wanted to distract the students with the length of their hair. Now that school was out for the day, Laurie began her end of the day ritual. Fussing with her hair always felt wonderful and often prompted her thoughts.

"Some of my students have no curiosity about anything," she said out loud, shaking her head again more vigorously. "It is just as my mentors have said." Looking skyward, she spoke to an imaginary face she made in the gray billowing clouds stacked above her. "I understand, Dorothy. It's the long loneliness for me that is coming, isn't it… the conflict leading to change?"

Laurie Flanagan had grown up in New York City. She had exchanged the crowded impersonal nature of that busy city for the isolation of the Oregon woods, and the slower pace of the small town of Horton. Laurie smiled as she remembered her rapid transformation and the clarity of the mission she now felt. Her inner circle of Irish Flapper friends had encouraged her to become a teacher and she went after her certificate with zeal. Finishing ahead of her class with boundless energy remaining, she had been unsettled on where to apply for work.

Laurie had astonished friends and family alike with her quick decision and abrupt departure from the comfortable life in New York City. She had found the cause of Women's Suffrage and immersed herself in it. Now, the words of her friends Sean and Andrew imploring her to rethink her "rash move," were only a distant memory. Her insistence on following in the footsteps of contemporary women who were making history in the Women's Suffrage Movement had at first been well received by her inner circle of friends. They were impressed by how passionately she expressed each woman's mission, tracing violent and non-violent methods, sometimes with tragic results and not all successful.

"No one will ever force feed me," she boasted, recalling women's suffrage events that had occurred in England before the war.

Near the end of her time in New York, Laurie's friends heard about a female leader of the Personalist Movement, Dorothy Day.

"A Distributionist society is what we need, a nation of small businesses all equal," Laurie told them with gusto. "Women must unite, like we did for the vote and spearhead change." Some time later, Laurie instructed them, as if they were children in her classroom, about Willa Cather, an American author who wrote a book about women pioneers. Finally, Sean had accused her of having a "Mentor of the Month." When the group heard about yet another inspirational leader of Women's Suffrage out West, Abigail Scott Duniway, they grew weary and began avoiding Laurie. Abigail had inspired the movement that granted women the right to vote in Oregon in 1912. Laurie began to feel a pull to leave New York and develop her own women's group. The distance that had grown between her and her friends made her decision to leave easier.

Once she arrived in Horton, Laurie corresponded regularly with women in the Sheridan women's group, organized by Flora Knickerbocker. Her dream to set up a chapter in Horton that would be devoted to the Third Way movement was getting closer.

Laurie felt the struggle of her students, she was sure, in a way that no one else in Horton or the Lake Creek Valley could. Each morning children arrived at school with their heads down, faces drawn, already fatigued from their morning chores on the farms and ranches in the Valley. It was their faces that Laurie saw regularly in her dreams. Her students worked hard just to be children. She had reported in letters to her friends Back East that her students were forced to grow up too fast to be individuals of contemplative thought. Something had to change in Horton, if she could only make it happen. If she lost her job she was sure she could carry on her mission somewhere in the Willamette Valley.

There seemed to be an unwritten rule in Horton that school ended before graduation. Many of the older, brighter students dropped out of school at crop time, never to return. No matter how hard she pleaded with them or their parents, the answer was always the same. If they were needed to bring in the crop, school must be delayed. They were unable to see the truth about the importance of education, as she saw it, in their isolated lives.

None of the families of the railroad workers or mill workers living in Horton could look beyond the surrounding hills either. At first, she had made house calls on many of the students living in and around Horton. From these visits, she learned the students had few books at home, and she felt resentment from the parents for her minimal homework assignments.

A letter to friends Back East requesting any books they could send, resulted in a trunk of books, many too advanced for the reading levels of her students. If you lived here, you were slaves to the weather and the Horton brothers, Laurie quickly concluded. The time to act had come.

The three Horton brothers owned much of the town and the sawmill, as well as part of the combined railroad enterprise. Laurie looked on them with suspicion as the major employer in the valley. In Laurie's mind, in Horton, like so many towns run by big companies with big ideas, it was always about making people work to feel their worth, never about nurturing personal creativity. If the work were here, her lost children would never leave.

She and fellow teacher, Mildred Persons, had made great strides. They had a school bus now instead of a wagon to bring the children in from the southern end of Lake Creek Valley. And, they had adjusted their school curriculum to be heaviest during the winter months, after all the crops were in. Changing other things however, was painfully slow.

Mildred had been the teacher at the nearby Alvadore School for many years. Reluctantly, she had responded to the Horton School Board's request to modernize all grade levels at their school. The reputation of the school at Horton soon began to soar and Mildred, now in her eighties, had welcomed Laurie's arrival and her youth and Irish energy with enthusiasm.

"Soon I must choose and begin their training," Laurie said softly, as she noticed the skies darkening overhead. If she started working with more than one student, surely there would be one to leave this place, to carry the torch of individual choice. She would teach them the full meaning of the Third Way. A nation of small businesses was the future, not large impersonal conglomerations of wealth. She remembered again that once out in the open, her Personalist beliefs would not be popular. But, she concluded, nodding her head and looking upward, she would meet them all head on, if that was how it had to be, "I must tame the lion from inside its mouth," she said to the dark clouds overhead. "The Third Way is coming and I have to prepare them."

The view from the doorway of the schoolhouse also gave her a good view of the hills around the town. Laurie drew in a breath; her thoughts about the blanket of distant green trees suddenly posed a conflict. A single tree was beautiful but the open spaces here and the fabric of so many trees together had given her a sense of beauty and freedom rather than confinement. Confused, she turned to leave, bumping into

Mildred who had been standing behind her, silently enjoying the view and the growing shadows.

"What were you saying, dear?" Mildred asked softly.

"Just thinking out loud about the future, that's all," Laurie replied. "Good night, Millie."

...

Sawing trestle timbers, cross ties, and rail planks out of raw logs was the main business of the Horton Mill. The waste wood left over however, posed a year-round fire hazard. An enormous teepee-shaped "Wigwam Burner" had been constructed to dispose of the waste wood. The burner stood like a rust-colored lighthouse next to the Horton mill. Standing four stories tall, it towered over every building in town. The burner covered the buildings with soot at times and started spot fires in the nearby forest during the summer. Fire, it seemed, was a constant companion of life in a sawmill town.

The burner was rarely watched during the day despite the showers of sparks that shot through the screen at the top. People tended to stay away from the sides of the burner as well, as the metal would glow orange from the heat, when the mill was running flat-out. A steam-powered conveyor carried every piece of wood without a purpose, up close to the top and deposited it through an open hole. Cut ends of water-soaked "green" wood, sawdust, chips, and bark, made one last ride to the top of the conveyer, entering the open hole, making a free fall to the fiery inferno below. To regulate the burner, metal side panels at ground level were removed until the smoke from the burner was fluffy white. More wood in the burner required more side panels to be removed. It was common for the last of the embers to remain hot at the bottom of the burner until morning. Soot-covered, red-faced mill worker, Toby Coalaski, tended the wigwam burner each evening. It was a thankless job, especially when a week's accumulation of ashes had to be removed. Nicknamed Coal by the mill jitney drivers, Toby worked late into the night most nights. Although the beehive shaped burner usually burned out during the early evening hours, Coal's responsibilities during the dry season included a fire watch until 2 a.m. Often, near the end of the day, Coal would enter the burner and push the last of the wood pieces that had escaped the inferno into a central pile, to speed things up, sending a huge shower of sparks skyward. It was the last colorful expression of normality the watchful community would see at the end of the day. A shower of sparks meant things were as they should be.

There was a walk-around distance everyone maintained to avoid being burned when the burner was hot. It was just outside the walk-around that Bull and Coal met regularly after dark on Friday nights, near the main door of the burner. Coal's homemade Black Pot moonshine was Bull's favorite. Coal handed the jar of pale liquid to Bull who drank eagerly, finally passing it back to Coal.

"You got it straight now, Coal?" Bull asked. "If there be trouble in town or any big shots from the railroad show up here, you make that smoke black for me, won't you?"

"Can do, boss," Coal nodded eagerly, as Bull gestured with his head toward a sack of apples, an essential element in Coal's homemade liquor. Coal grinned a near-toothless smile; his lack of front teeth proof that his decisions in important matters did not always demonstrate thoughtful restraint.

"I need to see that smoke, good and black, need it to drift up the creek for a signal. Keep it black for a couple of hours so I can see it from High Pass."

CHAPTER 7

THE NIGHT JOURNEY

How depressing, how tragic. After conquering what must have seemed at times an insurmountable challenge of terrain and nature's quirks of fate, to ultimately be terminated by the greedy indiscretions of men miles away...

—Earl Kelley, from *No Way to ~~Run~~ / Build a Railroad*

Late Friday Night, March 1, 1929

Tara and Rosie clung to each other in their mother's bed, finally falling asleep in the late evening darkness. All three of the Jack women had prayed unceasingly until midnight as showers of sparks rose upward from the wigwam burner, visible from their window. They began to feel strength just seeing the sparks rising to the heavens, as if each spark carried a prayer for Hiram Jack. Finally, when Polly could no longer see the sparks rising from the wigwam burner at the Horton Mill, she grew restless. Weary from worrying, it dawned on her that her restless thoughts led her in a circle of powerlessness.

Separating slowly from the girls, she rose, and stood over them, silently watching their rhythmic breathing. There would be no sleep for her tonight. Yawning, she continued to study them closely, pulling a blanket up and over their shoulders, as they lay tangled together in a loving embrace. Their peaceful slumber was a beautiful picture in the low lamp light, and she longed to return to the warmth of the communal comfort the girls offered, even asleep. Perhaps thoughts of them could somehow keep Hiram warm. Silently, she sent him her wish. She wondered what he was thinking about. Was he afraid? Did he know she would not rest until there was news of him?

Both girls were heavy sleepers and would not awaken for hours. Still uncertain what to do to find her husband, she walked to her favorite window and strained into the darkness, searching the blackness for inspiration. After several minutes she returned to the bedside where Tara and Rosie lay sleeping. Remembering the touch of the coarse wool that covered them, it was suddenly clear: she must act, now. If Hiram were outside without shelter, he wouldn't have a blanket. A plan began to take shape in her mind. She stood alone in the middle of the kitchen weeping in relief as she dressed. She would leave the girls alone in the house and hope to be back by daylight. After dressing warmly, packing blankets, some of the uneaten apple dumplings and some of Hiram's clothes, she left the house.

The frosty crunch under her feet and the March night chill, so typical of their mountain home this time of year, made her quicken her step as she walked briskly down to Horton. Her destination was Verin Palmer's log cabin.

Verin and Gray lived along the wooden tracks, at the east end of town. Polly knocked loudly, and then knocked again, finally pounding her fist on the door. After a long wait, Gray unlocked the door.

The knocking had sounded frantic as it echoed throughout the small cabin. Gray had jumped to his feet, an annoyed frown on his face. He stood motionless for a moment, listening, hoping whoever it was had gone away. When the knocking began again, he reached under the bed searching for his boots. When the persistent knocking became steady banging, Gray pulled his boots on quickly and stumbled toward the front door. Waiting for his mind to clear, he heard his grandfather stirring. He felt the cold, flattened coin in his pocket as he snapped one buckle of his bib overalls over one shoulder and onto the metal breast button.

Verin Palmer's feet landed hard on the wooden floor in the rear of the cabin with a "thump." He took in a deep breath, forcing himself awake, rubbing the stubble on his chin; he tried to make sense of what was happening. In the middle of a yawn, he pronounced, "I need a minute. Before you open that door, get a lamp up, so we can see who it is," Verin cautioned. "You been asleep, boy?" Verin asked as he caught up with

Gray near the door.

"Uh-huh," Gray replied. "Who's knocking out there, Grandpa?" Gray asked.

"Damned if I know, turn up the lamp and hand it over here," the grandfather replied.

"Mister Verin?" a familiar voice could be heard outside the door. "Mister Verin?" the voice repeated anxiously. "Please open the door," Polly urged.

There was silence for a moment. Then in the darkness, Gray heard his Grandpa's irritated voice behind him. "I'm a-coming, hold your britches. Don't move like I used too."

"Open the door, please," Polly pleaded again. "I need your help."

"We got a fire in the middle of winter or something?" Verin fumed.

Gray turned the dead bolt lock and slowly opened the door. He could feel his grandfather's heavy breath on his bare shoulder, behind him in the dimly lit room.

Polly burst through the open door. "I need you to go with me now and take a stroll up the grade," Polly said in the calmest voice she could manage.

"In the dark?" Verin asked.

"I've got some food and blankets here," Polly said, holding up the bundle she had carefully wrapped. She began to circle the room, obviously looking for something.

"Hold on now, what's this about?" Verin asked.

"Just get your coat," Polly said, barely able to control the quivering in her voice. "We have to get started," she stammered. "It may be a long night you see, and…and …"

At that moment Polly stopped talking, words frozen in her throat. Standing in the middle of Verin's sagging wooden floor, her body began to shake violently. She hid her face from them, turning away.

Verin gently took Polly's arm and escorted her to a kitchen chair. Once she was seated, he stood by, softly patting her head. "Take your time now, Mrs. Jack, and tell me."

Reassured by Verin's presence, Polly was soon able to speak again. "You know my Hiram come up missing today?" she began.

"Yes, I know," Verin responded. "I heard at the boarding house after the Gentry come in."

"I've got to find him tonight," Polly insisted. "He needs me."

"I'm going with the search party at first light," Verin said, calmly.

Polly looked at Verin, then at Gray with pleading eyes. "He could be hurt," Polly anguished, tears flowing down her cheeks. "The thought of him out in this weather, and us by a warm fire. We have to go now!" she said firmly.

Verin and Gray looked at each other. Verin nodded to Gray, who understood. Yawning, Gray headed to the back of the cabin to fetch both their hats and coats.

Following the wooden tracks out of Horton was not difficult with the kerosene lamp lighting their way. Gray and Verin both felt conflicted about trying to find Hiram Jack in the dark. While Verin pressed on ahead, cursing under his breath, Gray paused and looked back longingly, thinking of the warmth of the cabin.

They had sent Polly Jack back to her girls, arguing that they could do as well without her in the dark, and that Tara and Rosie needed her more right now. The men assured her that they would return to her immediately if they found any trace of her husband.

Gray began to think about other outings he had enjoyed with his grandpa, which were always an adventure. Gray quickened his pace to catch up. Verin's lantern swung to and fro, casting ghostly shadows on the tall trees that crowded them on both sides of the wooden tracks. As the men started to climb out of the valley, their feet made a hollow sound on the laminated rails. Soon, it started to rain.

Verin and Gray reached the first small turn in the wooden rails and paused to catch their breath. They were still a mile below the Big Bend turn in the grade, where the wooden tracks started an even steeper ascent to High Pass. Suddenly, there was a loud crash of breaking branches in the underbrush just below them. The noise continued with splashing sounds into the creek and up the hill on the other side. Although it was dark, Gray immediately felt brave and lunged into the darkness, in the direction of the creek. He soon stumbled, falling to his knees.

"Wait Gray! A man wouldn't make that kinda noise after dark," Verin called urgently, holding his lamp as high as he could. "It may be something much bigger, maybe a bear…" The words seem to catch in Verin's throat.

Gray called out loudly, "Mr. Jack, that you?"

"Don't go too far ahead, Gray," Verin warned. When there was no response, and against his instinct, he followed, down the bank toward the creek. The inky darkness under the giant fir trees enveloped him. "Gray! Get back here!" Verin roared. The mixture of potent odors, fresh turned earth, punkie wood, and rotten meat was overpowering. "Don't like the smell of this," Verin mumbled.

"I'm here Grandpa," Gray said, stumbling back to his Grandfather's side.

A loud metallic "snap" startled both of them, followed by a scream from Verin, "Oh, my God!"

In the dark, Gray was suddenly confused by what he saw. Verin began thrashing around in a circle, and sank to his knees. In the lantern light, Gray saw panic on his grandfather's face.

A steel-jawed bear trap had closed violently on Verin's ankle, crushing the old man's bones like dried twigs. Padlocked to a tree, the heavy forty-pound steel trap tethered Verin in a tight circle.

Gray dropped to his knees beside Verin, and could feel the cold teeth of the trap along with his grandfather's warm blood, which seemed to be everywhere. Soon, Gray's hands became sticky and he tried frantically to wipe them off on his shirt.

Verin had settled to his knees, still swearing under his breath. His head bowed to his chest, he slowly fell onto his side. A few moments later, he rolled onto his back and began thrashing in pain.

"Stupid! Stupid! Stupid!" he snapped. "Them Banks brothers didn't mark this leg trap. They're gonna pay!" Verin yelled. "By God, all eight of 'em are gonna pay! Gray, get this thing off me!"

Gray was stunned and unsure what to do. Finally unable to keep a hold on the trap as his grandfather squirmed, he spoke. "Hold still, it's digging in deep through your boot."

"I am holding still, damn it," Verin snarled. "I got no choice in the matter. It hurts like Hell.…I'll hold the lamp higher so you can see," Verin said, forcing the words. When Verin's leg was illuminated, the jaws of the trap were nearly closed on his ankle. Gray could see the two release levers, one on each side of the unforgiving device that held his grandfather. He began pushing on the release levers. Although he pushed harder and harder bouncing his weight on the levers, nothing happened.

Realizing he wasn't strong enough to depress the levers on both sides of the jaws at the same time, he began to panic. Verin and Gray needed help. Looking at each other for direction, it was clear, they both knew it. Verin, sensing Gray was feeling helpless, spoke calmly in a soft silky tone.

"Fetch that long stick there and stand on one side of the trap. I'll push down on the other side with the stick," Verin said slowly, trying to remain calm.

Gray responded quickly, regaining his composure. The stick Verin had seen was just outside the circle of light from the glowing lantern. Tripping on a blackberry runner in the dark, Gray fell face forward, onto an old blackened log, hitting his nose and chin. He struggled to breathe as he rolled off the log onto the soft ground. The smell and taste of raw dirt and blood filled his nose and mouth immediately. Both sensations were familiar from a previous accident.

Old memories, now triggered, flooded over him. Gray's father had made him hoe the garden one afternoon when he had planned to go fishing. In a hurry to save some daylight for fishing, he had worked quickly, and the dirt had turned over easily. Gray worked hard until the hoe handle broke. He had became extremely angry, and had kicked the short handle near the metal blade violently, falling down. When he had tried to stand, he realized the blade of the hoe was stuck in his foot. The blade had not sailed across the garden as he had expected. Instead, it had gone through his leather boot and penetrated into his foot. Gray had realized his mistake when the horrible throbbing pain had begun.

The awful stinging he felt had forced him to hop on one foot that day. Suddenly feeling dizzy and sick to his stomach, he had seen that the blade was imbedded deeply in the pad of his foot, just beneath his big toe. He sat down hard on the dirt to try to remove it. Unsuccessful, he had struggled to his feet that time, using the long broken shaft of the hoe handle as a crutch. After hobbling a few steps, the pain had became so unbearable that he fell. Frantically he had tried to pry the blade loose one last time, using the hoe handle to poke at the blade. When that failed, he had screamed for his mother, only to get no response. Standing again, leaning on the broken handle, he had tried to limp toward the house.

When his mother, Stella Palmer, heard his screams, she had come rushing out, drying her hands on her apron. Seeing his distress, she had run to Gray and tried to calm him. Touching his face with her hand, she found it cold, and he was perspiring profusely. Seeing the tears in his eyes and terror on his face, at first she had no idea what was wrong until he pointed to his foot.

"Don't struggle so," he could hear his mother saying, "We can think our way through this."

Struggling to stand in the dark, Gray began to search for Verin. His whole face throbbed, warm blood dripped steadily from his nose and mouth onto his shirt. He was dazed, and the lantern light seemed to be dancing in front of his eyes.

When Gray didn't reappear immediately, Verin called out to him urgently. "Come here now, Grayson, and help me." Gray struggled to his feet. Nearly tripping over Verin, he settled in beside him.

"Sweet Baby Jesus, boy," Verin exclaimed. "What happened to you?" he asked, raising the lantern. The lantern light revealed a grotesque sight: as near as Verin could see in the distorted light, Gray's face had two mouths. At first, Verin thought he was seeing double. The cut below Gray's mouth was as wide as his actual mouth. It was a nasty ragged cut exposing the roots of several teeth. Pieces of charcoal-like beard stubble stuck out of the wound in several places.

Dazed and desperate to help, Gray tried to talk but could only muffle the words, "I kin go back dun the grad and get hip, Grandpa." Gray slurped, spitting out a bloody mouthful of charcoal and dirt.

Verin realized Gray was so dazed by his fall he did not know how badly he had been injured. " No, Gray," he spoke reassuringly. "You can't leave me without a light."

Verin was nearly lost for words, shaken by his first view of Gray's face. "That bear will be back," he began again, collecting his thoughts. "It knows the trap is sprung, and knows there is food here. If it's an old sow, she's likely got cubs to feed; she'll be back. We have to stick together, Gray, so get this trap off me, so we can get ourselves back down the grade."

Verin's own consciousness was beginning to dim. He realized despite his discomfort, he would have to think for both of them now. His pain seemed to be subsiding.

"You got your 'kerchief, Gray," Verin had asked? Gray fumbled in his pocket, dropping his handkerchief near Verin's outstretched hand. "Sit down here and let me get a look-see at your face." A metallic clank from the Indian head penny surprised them both, as it fell out of his pocket and bounced off the jaws of the metal trap. "What was that?" Verin blurted impatiently.

"Your Indian cent," Gray mumbled. "Been smashed on the track."

The words had no sooner left his mouth than Verin roared. "Find that damn coin! Where is that stick?"

On his hands and knees, Gray located the tree limb, dragging it back to Verin. As Verin held the handkerchief to Gray's mouth with one hand, both began to feel the ground for the Indian penny. Gray's head began to clear and despite his pain, he began to feel better. He patted the earth around the trap looking for the Indian head penny. When Verin tried to help look for the flattened coin, he found that any twisting motions he made caused an immediate increase of pain and bleeding. Finally, Gray held up the Indian cent triumphantly.

Verin had managed to raise the wick of the kerosene lantern to get more light on their work. He decided he could use his weight to hold the spring down by leaning on the stick. He reasoned that with Gray standing on the other lever of the trap, he would have a free hand to wedge the jaws open and hold them there with the coin. They would have to push down mighty hard at the same time.

"Gray, you have to reach down and wedge the coin on its edge between the jaws when they open up."

"OK, Gampa, I'm ready," Gray said nervously, sensing time was running out for his grandfather. They had to get it right on the first attempt. He could see Verin fumbling to hold the stick over the spring release lever on his side of the trap.

"OK, gib it all the umph you got," Gray said with authority, despite the lisp from his injury. "Rebby?" Gray's jaw was set hard. "Now puch!"

Together, they began to apply pressure to the trap. "It's working!" Verin spoke triumphantly. "Now slide that coin in there and wedge it on the edge between two of the teeth." Cautiously, Gray bent down, making sure to keep his weight and both feet on the narrow release mechanism of the trap. "I think I got it," Gray said triumphantly.

"Great!" Verin replied. "We need something a little bigger than the coin now to wedge it open further," Verin whispered. "Don't want to lose what we gained." Verin clawed at the dirt around him until his fingernails turned over a small rock. Soon he had a good pile of rocks in all sizes. When the two of them pushed on the levers again, Gray placed the largest rock in the pile that would fit between the points of the jaws.

"All right, now: together, again," Verin said. As they both brought their weight down on the trap's release levers, Verin was able to turn his leg and slowly remove it, while avoiding touching the rock that held the jaws open. "Hey, it really worked!" Verin said, relief evident in his voice. "Careful now, easy does it," he grunted. We need to bind up my leg, and your mouth."

When they were ready, Gray helped his grandfather to his feet and together they struggled back up to the railroad grade. When Verin stumbled and began to moan with each step, Gray suggested they stop at the only shelter nearby, an abandoned dynamite shed. Built by the gandy dancers along the grade, the shed was locked, but no longer held any explosives. Gray had discovered the empty structure weeks before when Bull had rudely pushed him, the "stow-away," off the train. Noticing several loose sideboards, Gray had explored the inside.

Now, it would provide them rest and shelter from the rain, if he could force the door. Verin agreed. Gray squeezed through the loose boards as before and unlocked the door from the inside. Together they forced the heavy door open. Struggling to keep his grandfather upright in the pitch-black interior of the shack, they tripped over several buckets and tumbled into a pile of wet clothes on the floor, his grandfather falling on top of him.

"Son of a …" Verin said angrily.

When Verin's moans became intolerable an hour later, they agreed they could not wait for daylight to start home. Together, arm in arm, they struggled out the door, bringing several of the dirty shirts with them for bandages. Verin had insisted they turn the lamp low to make it last. When the lamp oil was nearly gone, they did their best to quicken their pace. They hobbled along in silence. Suddenly, two pale green eyes appeared on the tracks ahead, reflections from the dying lamp light. The eyes were directly in the middle of the tracks blocking their path.

"God, it's the bear!" Verin yelled.

...

Polly hadn't taken matters into her own hands initially, until after returning home. She was skeptical of Bull's explanation of the reason for her husband being missing and doubtful of Verin and Gray's chance for success without her. After she had pled with Verin to help find her husband, he had finally agreed to walk up the grade as far as possible until first light. Then, Gray would walk down one side and Verin the other, until they got back to Horton.

Verin had insisted Polly return home and leave the search to the men, and she had obeyed them initially, but on the way back home she quickened her pace, knowing she had to help them search for her husband.

She then quietly woke her girls, and the three of them left the house together. They saddled Scout, mostly by feel, in the low light provided by two kerosene lanterns. Tara snapped a lead bridle on the excited pony while Polly and Rosie packed the blanket bundle, placing additional food and water in the saddlebags.

They walked down the hill toward the grade. A layer of cold fog lay along the ground, slowing their progress. Tara and her mother walked ahead of Scout, carrying lanterns to light the path for the pony, while Rosie rode on Scout's back. If Hiram was injured and lying along the tracks, Polly knew she had to find him. She felt a new confidence: it's time to trust my instincts, she had decided.

Polly and Tara walked down the middle of the narrow wooden tracks, arm in arm, leading Scout. After an hour they stopped and rested near what they believed was the Big Bend turn in the grade. From here the going would be steeper. Despite a steady rain that started as they began to gain elevation, they were not shivering. Rosie, wrapped in a dark blanket, changed places with Tara and now led the way. She had been this far along the tracks many times. Only once had she dared to go farther, however, and never in the dark.

"We have to find your father and get him home," Polly announced, breaking the silence. "If he needs mending, we're the ones to do it, right girls?" Polly said confidently.

Suddenly they could see a solitary lantern light coming toward them. "Hello in the dark there," Polly yelled excitedly.

"Papa?" Rosie called, hopefully.

"Hiram! That you?" Polly said expectantly, holding both lanterns up high to shine ahead. There was silence, and then Verin's weak voice shocked them.

"It be Verin and Gray," Verin called back. "Were both no-account, and thought you was a bear! Gray here, hurt his face and my leg's bleeding real bad."

Dropping the lead rope on Scout, Polly and Rosie ran forward toward the fading lamp light. When they saw Verin and Gray they were horrified. Rosie put her hand over her mouth and had to look away. Polly held the light up to Gray's face, then down to Verin's leg. "Oh my, my," Polly said. "You two have been busy!"

Tara slid off Scout's back, bringing the pony up last. "Where's the bear?" she asked excitedly.

All thoughts of Hiram vanished as Verin's lamp went out. The four of them worked to get him up and onto Scout's back. Rosie had the task of leading the still-dazed Gray by one hand and holding one of their lamps with the other. Gray held a shirt from the shed to his face. Polly led Scout with one hand and held out the lantern in front with the other, lighting their way. Tara walked beside Scout, tightly holding on to Verin in the saddle. All together, they slowly trudged back to Horton, arriving at daylight. No one was waiting to welcome them or their parade of pain.

CHAPTER 8

THE PILGRIMS

This was the era when communities made their opportunities. And the undisputed leader of such communities was the mill owner. It was the mill owner who gained access to timber or stumpage that was harvested for saw logs. It was the mill owner who negotiated loans from bankers to finance the buildings, equipment, and payrolls. Therefore, the success of the community hinged on the financial influence of the mill owner. Consideration for bank loans at times was also determined by the steadfast reputation of his employees.

—Earl Kelley, from *No Way to ~~Run~~ / Build a Railroad*

February 28, 1929

Twin brothers and church builders, Earl and Mearl Keys, were ministers in the Pilgrim Holiness Church of Wisconsin. All winter they had been planning and organizing an aggressive church planting effort in Lane, Linn and Benton counties in their adopted state of Oregon. Finding Eugene much different than their hometown of Milwaukee, Wisconsin, the two believed themselves to be on an inspired mission for the Lord, in an unholy land. They had gone to the Eugene post office together that day. Earl had spun open the combination to their post office box while Mearl waited.

Simultaneously reaching for the large official-looking envelope, curled in the narrow box, they nearly ripped it in half in the ensuing struggle. The two brothers stood dumbfounded when they examined the contents. It contained two stock certificates, one for each of them: shares in the Horton Railroad. It took only a moment for the two to determine that between them their certificates were worth $500. The attached letter, signed by the Horton brothers, asked them to make an exception to their tent-meeting schedule, which was widely posted around the counties, and to hasten to Horton instead.

February 23, 1929

Dear brothers in our Lord,

Our combined families greet you and compliment you on your fine work for His kingdom. We believe that your ministry should be supported. Kindly accept our offering and consider our request for a favor.

We did not see our community of Horton, Oregon on your church revival schedule for this year.

As you may know, our church is being rebuilt, ever so slowly, following a fire last fall. We are hoping you will help us revive our "fundamental" roots and get the building project back on schedule. We would like to host you and a "revival of the faithful," in Horton at your earliest convenience. Will a meeting next month, in March of this year be possible? And, we will of course cover all your expenses, and more, while you are here in our fine community.

While the winter poses traveling difficulties, we are hoping the enclosed contribution to your ministry will compensate you.

We are all weary travelers on the Lord's highway. We wish to be inspired in our labors to new heights.

> *Your servants in Horton,*
>
> *Joseph, Andrew, and Peter Horton, and families*

Having no idea where Horton, Oregon was, they consulted a trusted parishioner, from whom they learned that the closest major town was Junction City in Lane County. Locating a Sanborn Fire Insurance map of the area, they were still unable to locate the tiny lumber community. Puzzled, they began to wonder if their certificates were genuine. When they consulted a vice president of the First National Bank of Eugene, they were referred to Willard Spencer, one of the chief stockholders in the railroad who was then living at the Eugene Hotel.

The three men sat facing each other in the plush lobby that still smelled of fresh paint. Examining the letter and the stock certificates, with false compassion for the mission of the Keys brothers, Willard nodded and smiled.

"I see the Horton brothers think the town needs…" searching for words, Willard finally settled on, "motivating by a higher power," he said with a sly smile. Not a religious man, but seeing a business opportunity, he gave a short history of the project to the Keys brothers. Finally, he asked them a question.

"Well, gentlemen, what can I do for you?"

"Can you tell us what the best way is to get to Horton?" Earl asked.

"And," added Mearl, "Will we need horses, Mr. Spencer?"

Willard laughed. "You can certainly get there by horse but what you will need most is a pair of wading boots!"

The two brothers looked at each other, now uncertain as to what they were getting themselves into.

"The road going in is not much," Willard continued, realizing as he spoke that he would have to make his own trip to Horton soon. Locating Horton on the road map he retrieved from his hotel suite, he traced the route from Eugene.

"Not much traffic in the winter because the road is twisty, washes out, and there is some unreliable bridgework," Willard cautioned. The Keys brothers nodded, recognizing Junction City on Willard's map and noticing Horton was west in the Coast Range some 25-30 miles by road. Next, Willard gave the twins a brief estimate of the prosperity that was assured for the whole Lake Creek Valley once lumber began flowing into the Willamette Valley over the shortcut through Coast Range. The phrase "assured prosperity," were the words the Keys brothers needed to re-think their schedule; Willard was a good salesman.

"The company believes in your mission gentlemen, that is clear," Willard said, skillfully shifting gears to his own mission. "I know you will encourage the folks there to keep supporting the railroad we're...

rather, they're building," he said, correcting his choice of words. "Like your mission work, the railroad needs financial support to be successful. We're entering the final phase of construction. An inspired push to finish can't hurt." Willard did not want to say more about the financial picture of the Horton Railroad, which he knew was in crisis. If the Horton brothers thought they could squeeze a few more dollars out of the locals, he was all for it. "Perhaps, you can bless the project properly while you're there?" Willard asked.

"Of course," the brothers said simultaneously. Pulling the necessary pieces together for the Horton stop would be a challenge during the winter, the twins agreed, but they were satisfied that their invitation to Horton was valid. "It is a sign from the Lord!" Earl declared with confidence, holding the certificate to his chest.

"He will provide!" Mearl replied, holding his own certificate aloft. It had been a hard time for the ministry's treasury with the rising unemployment in their home base of Eugene. The post-war economy had not prospered everywhere. Sadly, the twins' unique ability to create jealousy among the husbands of middle-aged women who attended their church-building services had continued to haunt the ministry's success.

CHAPTER 9

THE PRISONS

Running roughshod over the rights of others went mostly unchallenged or unquestioned. Of the aforementioned characteristics, the only one really applicable to the Horton-Junction City railroad was, in a minor degree, the last point mentioned—intimidation. "Railroading" is a still popular descriptive phrase for domineering, aggressive intrusive practices, a self-explanatory word coined in that era.

−Earl Kelley, from *No Way to ~~Run~~ / Build a Railroad*

Saturday, March 2, 1929

On Saturday morning, the day after Hiram disappeared, Bull and a group of volunteers rode the Gentry up to the bunkhouse near the end of the completed section of the tracks, ten miles from Horton. When Hiram could not be found, the group reluctantly spread out in the pouring rain on either side of the tracks, near the recent grade blasting from the day before. After searching the area, they worked their way back down the grade toward Horton for several miles.

Bull left the group, promising to pick them up at the Big Bend turn so they could ride the Gentry the last few miles back to Horton, at the end of the day. Having volunteered for what appeared to be the most difficult assignment, Bull climbed back into the cab of the Gentry and steamed to the end of tracks further up the grade. From there he would still have a half-mile walk up the unfinished grade to reach the summit of High Pass.

He had left with the blessing of the others, none of whom had enthusiasm for climbing to the summit in the rain. When they were out of sight, Bull pushed the throttle of the Gentry down as far as it would go and raced to the end of the tracks. There he left the Gentry, and walked the last half-mile to the future trestle crossing at High Pass crevice.

After the climb, Bull was breathing heavily. He stood at the top, looking across the rickety bridge that would soon be replaced. Then, he looked down cautiously into the crevice.

It had been a simple plan. Two weeks had passed since Bull had convinced one of the Bear Creek surveyors, working from the other end of the project, to cross the shaky bridge from the east side of the crevice and begin site and grade testing for Hiram Jack's trestle bridge. Both men agreed that someone had to inspect the walls on either side of the crevice to see if they would support trestle footings. It was decided that Seymour Purvis, the surveyor, would be lowered down slowly by rope to make the needed inspection. Bull, the bigger and stronger of the two, was the easy choice to pull up the lighter man when the inspection was completed.

Seymour watched as Bull tied a rope around a cedar stump conveniently located near the edge of the crevice rim.

"Plenty strong enough rope and a good knot," Bull said convincingly, pulling at the rope knot he had tied around the stump. Together, they fashioned a harness out of a pair of leather Timber Faller's chaps that Seymour could sit in comfortably.

Finally, Seymour wrapped himself in the makeshift swing and pronounced cautiously. "Feels safe enough."

"It's heck for stout," Bull replied with a smile. Looking quickly down into the canyon below, Bull estimated the distance to the bottom to be more than one hundred-fifty feet, well beyond the end of the rope they had. There would be no way for Seymour to go all the way down; he would have to be pulled back up and out of the crevice.

"Don't look down if it bothers you," Bull advised. "Give me a shout and I'll start reeling you up when you're done."

At the end of the tether, Seymour swung back and forth across the rock face, hammering here and there, looking at the rock samples he dug from the wall, while Bull waited impatiently. Bull's fear of heights kept him from watching the surveyor work. It was taking too long and Bull began to pace back and forth several feet back from the edge of the crevice. Finally, Seymour was finished but the echo coming up the canyon announcing this fact sounded like, "*cold.*"

"Alright, alright," Bull muttered under his breath, as he began to strain at the rope. "Next time wear your coat if you're cold, you fool."

When Bull extracted the man up the fifty feet of rope, Seymour was so excited he couldn't speak. Instead, he began to gesture wildly, like someone possessed. Bull was out of breath and sweating profusely, having pulled the fellow up by hand. Bent over at the waist, trying to regain his breath, he did not see Seymour's arm waving and finger pointing in the direction of the crevice. As Bull gasped for air, the surveyor grabbed him, trying to pull him back, closer to the ledge. Seymour's inability to speak annoyed Bull.

"Speak your mind," he said, pulling his arm away. He had no intention of spending more time looking down the one hundred-fifty foot to the bottom of High Pass crevice. Disgusted, he scooped up Seymour's coat and threw it too him.

"You were no help, Seymour," Bull said angrily. "I did all the work; quit your complaining. Next time, wear your damn coat!"

Assuming Seymour was jumping up and down to warm himself, merely complaining about the cool damp breeze that drifted up the canyon, or his task of swinging around at such height, Bull's mood on the whole experience was souring.

"It's there," Seymour finally choked out. "A vein, just out of sight, under the overhang," he stammered. "Not cold…gold! It's a narrow band imbedded in crystal quartz, fifty feet down the canyon wall," Seymour added excitedly. "I swear it's gold, you can't miss it!"

Bull muffled the man's voice with his hand over his mouth, as if someone could overhear. "You don't know what you're talking about," Bull scoffed.

"I do know what gold looks like," Seymour countered.

"Need an assay to say for sure," Bull interjected, still doubtful.

"I done some road survey work, near the top of Fairview, not more than fifty miles to the southeast," Seymour began. "I know they say more money was spent down in Bohemia lookin' for gold than was ever made, but this vein's as rich as any I've seen."

The surveyor continued telling his story as Bull began to listen intently. "When the mines started to play out six-months ago, I was let go and drifted back toward Cottage Grove. I panned enough gold flakes from Sharp's Creek to stake me, and then I headed north." Bull finally raised his hand, letting Seymour know that he should keep his voice down. "This is still gold country," Seymour added.

Bull learned over the next few minutes that investigating the rubble in the blasting along the grade at High Pass had been Seymour's secret preoccupation since being hired by the railroad. Seymour had said he could hardly believe no one else was prospecting after the blasting. He told Bull that he camped by himself, rarely seeing anyone for days. He hadn't even bothered to pick up his paychecks, which, he was sure, were being kept for him. At some point in the conversation, Bull decided Seymour was the perfect man to begin mining the strike, and that he would likely not be missed.

Bull demanded an ore sample for assay to be convinced that it was gold, and Seymour reluctantly agreed to make repeated trips down to the vein until Bull was satisfied. The two developed a regular routine over the next two weeks with Seymour doing the mining, camping out-of-sight on the east side of the crevice. Bull agreed to bring him food daily and whatever else he needed on his daily runs up from the bunkhouse during the week. Soon buckets with ore began to stack up. Finally, after several days of mining, Seymour began to grow impatient.

"Now, Seymour, be patient," Bull had said. "You know a formal assay that is good is a hard secret to keep. Your share is safe enough, we're splitting the buckets half and half." Recalling his experience with claim jumpers down in the Bohemia Mining District, Bull's words struck a chord of truth with Seymour.

"Hard luck miners will swarm all over the grade and interrupt the rail building, too," Seymour replied thoughtfully. "Guess we might as well get a good lode out before the assay."

During the second week, Bull devised a counter-balance pulley system with rocks, to make his job easier as he hoisted up the surveyor-turned-miner. A second, thinner rope for just the ore buckets allowed for fewer heavier pulls for Bull and it allowed Seymour to remain in the harness at all times.

By building footholds, and then a cave-like opening, Seymour was able to explore the quartz vein deeper into the hard rock wall. Unfortunately, water constantly dripped from the walls of the mine and flowed down the side of the crevice, one hundred feet below to Swartz Creek. Soon, water in the bottom of the new mine opening was ankle deep. It became slippery, dangerous work and Seymour began to complain that he needed better boots and more dry clothes. "I'm doing all the work," he told Bull, finally.

Bull had no intention of going down to work the mine himself unless it proved to be the only way to extract the gold. Since it was another hundred feet to the bottom of the crevice, and he was afraid of heights, Bull continued to insist that Seymour wear the rope harness at all times, even though the mine was now several yards deep into the rock face.

"The vein is getting larger," Seymour reported one afternoon.

Bull counted the ore buckets daily. When they began to fill up the dynamite shed near the top of the grade, Bull knew he was the luckiest man alive. As supervisor, it had proven an easy task to keep his crews away from the shed.

Near the end of the second week, Seymour began to grow distrustful of Bull. One day, when Seymour objected to going back down into the mine, an argument erupted between the men. Finally, Bull agreed to have the ore assayed immediately. As part of the bargain they struck however, Bull suggested that Seymour retrieve a large nugget he had dug from the wall of the mine the day before. "It's your nugget, all yours," Bull had said. Bull's sudden generosity sealed the deal. "If the strike is as rich as we think, then we'll know we got something with your big nugget. We'll put the claim in your name if you want," Bull had said, with his widest smile. Seymour was touched by this outpouring of generosity from Bull. He was eager to have his name on a real lode gold mine claim.

As Seymour was lowered over the side of the crevice one last time, he failed to notice a minor unraveling of the leather seat of his safety harness. A predictable malfunction of the harness followed, and soon he was free falling. Flailing his arms and shaking his fist at Bull, Seymour rapidly descended head over heels. His last thought as he passed the mine opening, was that Bull Kelly would get all the gold now. There was little time for other thoughts, as he fell the remaining hundred feet to his death.

Bull could not watch the "accident" unfold. He had but one thought: it was time for a new miner.

When grade master Hiram Jack insisted on making final measurements himself for the bridge footings to be cut by the Horton Mill the following week, Bull could not see why he should refuse him. Hiram had discovered the rope and pulley system on Friday morning. Concluding that someone else was working on the crevice crossing, Hiram had intended to inquire why he had not been told. The next time he saw Bull however, he was in no shape to ask or even defend himself. After the blasting, Bull found Hiram covered with debris from the explosion and only partially conscious. It had been easy to persuade him to put on the miner's harness. Using hand signals and shouting into Hiram's ear, Hiram finally understood he still had work to do.

After inspecting the lift system and the hastily-repaired harness, and finding it adequate to support his weight, Hiram allowed himself to be lowered down against the weight of the counterbalance pulley system. After descending fifty feet, Hiram's head began to clear. He saw the entrance to the mine. Puzzled by an apparently man-made opening in the rock, he waited for his eyes and brain to adjust. Constrained by the safety harness, he removed it without thinking and entered the mine. It was then he heard a faint grinding noise and noticed the metal bucket bumping down the canyon wall above. His safety harness was gone. A note in the bucket simply read:

> *You and me are now partners. Fill two buckets with ore every day and we will get along fine. If you're short one of the buckets, I'll cut your ration of food and water.*
>
> *I need you to work the mine for two weeks. You can always jump if my terms are too harsh. Yell if you want, but best to save your energy for the work. Soon you will be back with your family with enough gold for you and them to forget where it come from. You will thank me. You have my word.*
> —*Bull*

Back in Horton, Coal remained alert to danger for Bull. At 2:00 PM on Saturday, a lone rubber tire found its way onto the conveyer feeding the wigwam burner. Thick black oily smoke billowed out of the burner at first, and then dark slinking snakes appeared to rise above the treetops around Horton—an easterly slither. Carried by the afternoon breezes, sweeping up through the Lake Creek Valley, the signal smoke drifted slowly up Swartz Creek, as planned. Arriving at the Big Bend turn in the grade an hour later, the black band hovered briefly then pushed on, directed by the prevailing southwestern wind, blowing in from the Pacific Ocean at the higher elevation. Coal had heard something that would make trouble for Bull: a conversation between Andrew and Joseph Horton. Someone from the railroad was coming, someone named Willard Spencer.

Willard Spencer was a man who cared little for other people or their problems. He felt out of place as he looked around the uncomfortable company house of the missing grade master. He sat in Polly Jack's kitchen, watching the Jack girls put away newly-washed laundry, and as they worked, he watched Polly. His top hat lay perfectly level above his long overcoat, which he carefully folded and placed over the back of the room's only armchair. As a major stockholder and member of the Horton Railroad Board of Directors, he had several things on his mind. His reputation as a tough no-nonsense businessman was well known to insiders. Often choosing to stay out of the limelight, he was content to wield his power behind the scenes, until now. The Horton Railroad was running out of money. He had suggested in a closed-door session with Joseph Arnold, his boss, that they do a full inspection of the project for its salvage value before Arnold called for a vote on shutting it down.

Willard received Polly's "desperate message," dropped off by a delivery truck driver who happened to be leaving Horton for Eugene on Saturday morning. Having read the letter several times while waiting for the water level to fall at the floating log bridge just outside of Horton, Willard realized he had a more delicate assignment than he had anticipated. He cursed himself for arranging the short notice salvage inspection visit.

What did this woman think he could do about her missing husband, gone for only one day? Well, no matter, he thought to himself. He would be done with her and his business soon, and be back in Eugene by the middle of the week.

Willard had decided to meet the wife of the missing man first, before giving the bad news to Bull Kelley and the Horton brothers. He would hear her out and decide if she intended to make trouble. The Gentry would not be in for hours, he'd been told at the Horton Store, so he had time. He also decided he would set up the tour with Bull first then meet with the Horton brothers, owners of the mill. He would stay a few nights at the boarding house to make sure they understood what was at stake, and then get back on the unreliable road to Eugene.

Gazing at Polly, who was not unattractive, Willard's attention began to wander. He had heard her request for immediate dismissal of Bull Kelly if her husband could not be found during the search that day. What interested him most at the moment, however, was the pan of Huckleberry muffins that Polly had just removed from her oven. He was visibly annoyed when she offered the first hot muffins to her daughters instead of to him. Her message was unmistakable; her priority was her family and not his comfort.

Polly had occupied her time with baking, moving rapidly from one task to another in her kitchen. She told herself she needed to stay busy. When Willard arrived, she was surprised and pleased with such a rapid response from the railroad company. She composed herself, already sure of what she wanted from him.

"More coffee, Mr. Spencer?"

"No, thank you," Mrs. Jack. "I would like a muffin, if you don't mind, and I would take an extra for later," he said, forcing a smile.

"Of course," Polly replied.

After a brief conversation, it was clear that Polly Jack would be a problem for Joseph Arnold, the chief investor in the railroad. Perhaps, she would back away from her demand of firing Bull with a small incentive Willard thought.

"Mrs. Jack, may I call you Polly?" he asked.

"Mr. Spencer, my friends do call me Polly," she said with a forced smile. "I am pleased that you would ask and not assume," Polly continued, "and, since you have asked my permission, it is given."

Willard took a deep breath.. "As you can see we are deeply concerned about your husband," he began. "That is why I am here," Willard lied. "Would there be any other reason why he would not come home as expected?" Willard asked.

"Well, no, I don't think so!" Polly replied, stunned at the question.

"The company will make every effort to assist in the search. We have a perfect record you know, for the project here in Horton," Spencer continued. "You must know however, that we are directed by men who want results, and we are way over time here for completion. My approach toward the search will be intense but brief, and then we must get everyone back to work. In cases like this, there is usually a favorable outcome."

Polly walked across the room and gazed out the window and down toward Horton. "What will happen to us if Hiram doesn't come home?" she asked. When Willard didn't answer, she turned back to face him. He had put on his coat and hat and stood in silence.

"One thing at a time," he said, walking toward the door. Turning and tipping his hat to her, he said coldly, "Good day, Mrs. Jack, let us know at the office if you find him. Perhaps a small amount of financial compensation is due if he isn't found, but I cannot promise you."

Polly sat in silence in the dimming afternoon light of her kitchen, numb and unable to rise, after he left. He said it would be up to me to find him, she recalled. Finally, trying to make sense of her situation, she reached out into the air, pointing her finger at the no longer present Willard Spencer. "You are an impostor, Mr. Spencer," she said aloud.

She called the girls to her. Hugging them close, she held on until they objected. Finally, she released them, as they fidgeted for freedom.

Sunday, March 3, 1929

Polly felt alone and isolated when news of the failed search came to her from an exhausted Verin Palmer late Saturday night. He had insisted on going out again, despite his injury, to participate in the search for Hiram. He was limping heavily when Polly greeted him with a hug.

"Please come in and sit a spell, and tell us the news," Polly said, doing her best to sound hopeful. She had prepared some venison stew and, with a little coaxing, Verin soon seated himself at the Jack's table and began to eat. The silence that followed told Polly her husband was still missing. She swallowed hard and waited. When Tara realized that silence meant but one thing also, she began to cry. Polly reached out and drew her close. Soon both girls needed the comforting arms of their mother. As Verin ate, Polly watched his powerful arms and considered the stamina he displayed despite his injury, trying to gather strength for herself from him.

He had insisted on being dropped off at the Big Bend Turn, thinking Hiram must surely be closer to Horton than High Pass. Directing the search of the lower end of the grade, he had remained on the tracks all morning sitting and listening, and wondering what could have happened. As the searchers arrived from the upper end of the grade, he directed them down to the edge of Swartz Creek to look for Hiram's tracks in the soft mud and sand along the water's edge.

"I was sure he would go downhill and follow Swartz Creek out if he couldn't climb up to the grade," Verin began. "We checked the whole downhill side of the grade, Mrs. Jack," he said, disappointment clearly present in his voice. "It is a mystery where he went off to. Bull's convinced he is not around the bunkhouse. We plan to keep looking, though," Verin reassured her. "We need to check above the grade as soon as possible," he said, trying again to give the Jack women some hope. "Seems odd he would go uphill if he was injured, but, maybe he…" Verin paused, unable to think of a hopeful way to conclude his thoughts.

"Maybe he what?" Polly asked, a look of uncertainty on her face.

"Maybe he did go downhill and fell in," Verin said reluctantly.

After Verin left, Polly sat by the window, unaware that tears had begun to flow down her face again.

Wet, salty pathways now streaked her face, drops falling finally onto her apron. Drying her eyes, out of habit she was surprised to notice her apron was wet with her tears. She gazed at the pane of glass. In the daylight, the view was distorted slightly by the imperfections in the leaded glass. What would Hiram want me to do now, she asked herself? Hiram's words, that had earlier irritated her, returned, "Use it up, wear it out, make it do or do without," she recalled him saying. She focused on the last part of it: "make it do or do without." Was there some instruction for her in preparing to do without him, she wondered? She had to start thinking about their future. She forced the thoughts to emerge and began to make a list.

Polly began to consider possible resources. She hoped to never again see the cold and unfeeling Willard Spencer. She knew she could not expect any assistance from him, although he did hint at some financial help. To him, I will always be "Mrs. Jack," she said to herself—never more than a business expense. She could appeal to the Horton brothers, but they all had families, too, and she knew they were heavily invested in the mill and the town, as well as their railroad. Mill people came together when something like this happened, she remembered. Maybe the families of the mill and railroad workers would stand up for her in some way. She wondered how long they could remain in the company house. Finally, she realized that her girls needed to go to bed and she methodically began her evening routine.

CHAPTER 10

THE COUNCIL OF COMFORTERS

Inherent in the pioneers' nature was consideration for others' welfare and happiness. The idea was, there was some inconvenience or imposition in the world they lived in that required a softer kind of council.

−Earl Kelley, from *No Way to ~~Run~~ / Build a Railroad*

Several of the women from Horton had planned to visit the Jack home on Sunday, following the announcement of the failed search. Molly Bond, owner of the boarding house, and both teachers from the Horton School had met at the boarding house late Saturday. All three came to the Jack house knowing their visit was the most important thing they could do for Polly. The women arrived mid-morning Sunday with baked bread, smiles and hugs for each of the Jack women. Their cheerfulness felt at first out of place to Polly, but, after a while, she welcomed their lifting of the veil of grief the Jack house had been covered in. They asked Polly to repeat all she had heard about the results of the search. The visitors knew there would be relief in retelling the story, the results of which they had already heard.

While Polly recounted what Verin had told her, the trio began a systematic straightening of Polly's home. When Polly repeated the details of her rescue of Verin and Gray in the early morning hours the day before, she began to feel more hopeful. "Men," Laurie said, shaking her head, "what they won't get into." A polite laugh by everyone present continued to brighten the mood.

Over the next hour, each woman added words of admiration for Polly's efforts to find her husband. "You have done all you can possibly do!" Laurie insisted.

"Please sit here, Polly," Mildred said, rising from her chair and pointing to it. "We are here to take care of you."

Polly's shoes were carefully removed once she was seated. Mildred found a blanket, warmed it on the Jack's wood stove, and wrapped Polly in it. Polly sat down, exhausted, and immediately began to relax. She needed these comforters more than she could express. Encircled by the women, she felt her strength returning. Their continuing reassurances amidst happy and spirited conversation, was like music for her. As she let herself into their care and comfort, soothing thoughts of a joyful presence beyond her visitors filled her heart.

Laurie held Polly's hand, gently massaging her fingertips while Mildred massaged Polly's tired feet. Molly cut the baked bread that the group had brought and they all began eating and drinking tea. The house was filling with the scent of comfort and the sounds of sincerity that Polly would never forget. As Polly repeated the events of the visit by Willard Spencer the day before, Molly sat on the arm of the chair with her arm around Polly's shoulder. When Polly began weeping unexpectedly, the group grew silent. As her body recoiled with each sob, they let her cry, each one touching her.

The girls, playing in the next room, became alarmed and rushed to comfort their mother. With the three Jack women in the middle, the comforters encircled them, and together they softly cried.

CHAPTER 11

WHEEL of DESTINY

Without the convenience of today's mobility in transportation and equipment, one cannot help but stimulate admiration for the courage of the Oregon Pioneers in commencing such a vast and dangerous journey across the prairie, completed in less than one year. And, no less the fortitude of their children, in the current project, which continued over a five-year period.

–Earl Kelley, from *No Way to R̶u̶n̶ / Build a Railroad*

Monday Morning, March 4, 1929

The Horton school house had two rooms and an adjoining wood shed. Near the middle of one side, an iron potbelly stove had been installed, tended by assigned students during the long winter school days. Mrs. Mildred Persons had grades one through seven in one room and Laurie taught grades eight through twelve in the other. The excellent reputation of the improved school curriculum was a source of pride to the community, with students attending from throughout the Lake Creek Valley. The new, bright yellow school bus had also boosted enrollment, as students no longer had to travel back and forth in a tarp-covered wagon.

Mondays were assembly days: the teachers alternated planning the program for the morning. Often the children's favorite movies were shown. The 1925 silent movie, "The Wizard of Oz," was favored over the older swashbuckler movie, "The Thief of Baghdad," by a popular request of two to one. Today, after the movie, Laurie was continuing her lesson on United States history and westward expansion. Adding something she hoped would bring her topic to life, she planned a visit by a real pioneer. She wanted the individual accomplishments of the pioneers to inspire all the students.

Verin Palmer arrived, anxious to participate in the history lesson for several reasons. He planned to share a story from of his boyhood journey when he walked across the Oregon Trail, and introduce a related math contest. Secondly, he wanted to clear-up inaccurate rumors that were circulating about the injury-filled night in the woods and his version of what had really happened.

The current rumor explaining his leg injury had changed significantly as the news spread around Horton and among the students. Interestingly, none of the rumors included the bear trap any longer, only the bear, which had never been seen by the two. The current version was that Verin had survived an attack by a bear and that Gray had frightened it away by biting it back, receiving his facial injury in the ensuing struggle. Finally the Jack girls, Tara and Rosie, had arrived just in time to help them both escape in the dark.

Hobbled by his ankle injury from the bear trap on Saturday, Verin entered the room walking stiff-legged, chin high, with pride evident in every step. His injured ankle was concealed from view. The students gasped at the sight of him, their mouths dropping open in surprise: Verin was wearing his oldest, wide-brimmed hat and leather gloves, a tattered leather vest over a blousy red muslin shirt and dusty denim jeans. A pair of tall leather moccasins that he had laced above his ankles had replaced the boots he normally wore. Over his denim pants were a pair of worn leather chaps. He had come in costume, dressed as a pioneer, looking the part of a true traveler of the Oregon Trail. The students were delighted! To everyone's surprise, he was rolling an old, worn-looking wooden wagon wheel with an iron rim. The old wheel made a grinding noise against the wooden floorboards of the classroom.

"This here wagon wheel," Verin began, "is the only remaining piece from my folk's Prairie Schooner." Verin let the students examine the wheel as he talked. "Old and rusty now," Verin said. "I thought I might throw it away. Then, I got to thinking about what this here wheel could say if it could talk. It's not much good for anything, now. But if it could talk, what on earth would it say?"

The question hung in the air as Verin began to ask other questions. "How many people walked or rode the Oregon Trail," he asked the students?

"Half a million," a sharp seventh grader replied.

"Good," said Verin. "That's one point for the younger kids. You might win the prize today."

"What prize?" someone asked. Suddenly, with a contest and prize hanging in the air, all the students began to talk at once and both teachers raised their hands for quiet.

"You older kids," Verin continued, "What year did the Trans-continental Railroad get completed?"

Rosie yelled, "1869."

"Correct, one point for the older kids. Now, you younger kids," Verin continued, "What was it like walking the trail?" No one was quite certain.

Verin turned the wagon wheel toward him, rolling it around in place, knocking first on a spoke, then on the hub. "Let's ask the wheel; it was there," he informed them. "Let's all be quiet so we can hear what it says."

The room grew quiet as Verin tapped the wheel hub with a six-stroke knock. Pretending to get its attention, he knocked again, as if the wheel needed to be awakened from a long slumber. He began listening intently, his head bent down to the wheel, and a cupped hand on the back of his ear, nodding occasionally.

"How long was the Oregon Trail?" he asked the wheel.

"The Oregon Trail was 2000 miles long," Verin replied in a deep voice, speaking for the wheel. "Some people walked it barefoot!"

"You don't say," Verin exclaimed, returning his voice to normal, nodding his head in approval toward the wheel and then the students. "Did I hear you right?" he asked the wheel again. "The Indians were mostly helpful, not troublemakers to the immigrants? The biggest problems were sickness, lack of preparation, and gunshot wounds, you say?"

"Well, it's a wonder we made it, then!" Verin concluded thoughtfully. Turning to face the combined classes, he asked the students another question. "Why did people come to Oregon?"

There were many answers, but after a while the students began to grow restless. Finally, Gray suggested they just ask the wheel. Everyone laughed. Verin brought the discussion to a close with his summary.

"The Oregon Trail was a tough road to follow, not like now. Once some folks done it though, and sent back word that a wagon could make it, other people got the idea. Pioneers were dreamers, but sometimes had to leave their dreams along the way. Our neighbor back then, and some that came later, got here with nothing and had to be taken in by other folks that were luckier. We learned to take care of each other. We wanted everyone to make it. Everyone had a job, everyone was important. A gamble for ground—land—for my family, made the risk reasonable."

As he spoke he made a dramatic grabbing motion, reaching toward the students. "A lot of folk Back East told us we were crazy, that we'd die along with our dreams. Making a fresh start, making a change, always costs somebody something. Land was even free for a while. Why not reach out and grab some for yourself, do something brave."

Verin went back to discuss the contest further. "Today, your assignment will be to decide the total number of times this here wheel turned around going those 2000 miles. Each class should work together and tell Miss Laurie here the answer, then you get the prize of bear jerky I brought. I'll leave the wheel right here next to the stove...and, no asking the wheel!"

The students laughed again. As Verin departed, he said. "We never saw no bear, but we did tangle with a bear trap!"

The room began to buzz with excitement again as the students studied the wheel with renewed interest. Soon they were recalling facts from the lesson and starting their calculations. Rosie and Gray's class of 8th graders were victorious.

David Hascall The Longest Wooden Railroad

CHAPTER 12

THE DREAM

David Hascall The Longest Wooden Railroad

The Man with a Hoe

Bowed by the weight of centuries he leans
Upon his hoe and gazes on the ground,
The emptiness of ages in his face,
And on his back, the burden of the world.
Who made him dead to rapture and despair,
A thing that grieves not and that never hopes,
Stolid and stunned, a brother to the ox?
Who loosened and let down this brutal jaw?
Whose was the hand that slanted back this brow?
Whose breath blew out the light within this brain?

Is this the Thing the Lord God made and gave?
To have dominion over sea and land;
To trace the stars and search the heavens for power;
To feel the passion of Eternity?
Is this the dream He dreamed who shaped the suns
And marked their ways upon the ancient deep?
Down all the caverns of Hell to their last gulf
There is no shape more terrible than this--
More tongued with cries against the world's blind greed--
More filled with signs and portents for the soul--
More packed with danger to the universe.

–Edwin Markham

Tuesday Evening, March 5, 1929

For the first few days, Hiram Jack did as requested, even though he knew that Bull would likely not live up to his word. It had always been about working hard, Hiram thought. He wondered what sort of story Bull had spread around Horton about his disappearance. He didn't know many of the crew very well. Would they look for him? Maybe, maybe not. Finally, he settled on the one he was most certain would look for him, Polly. It brought a smile to his face; no one knew her the way he did. Briefly, he wondered if he could endear himself to Bull if he filled more buckets than Bull had demanded. There was nobility in doing exactly what you were told, and exceeding expectations. Hard work was good for the soul. If you labored under an agreement, you were due your pay. There was honor in it, a code. But, after a few hours he grew weary from wearing wet dirty clothes, he wanted to end his misery any way he could. When he examined his aching, calloused hands Tuesday evening, the first thoughts of despair washed over him. He imagined that his hands and body were covered with a wet disease-laden scum that made him a castaway, an unwanted, smelly creature. The certainty of his continued suffering was beginning to suffocate him—crowding out any rational thoughts—giving him strange ideas.

At the end of the day, Hiram sat slumped forward, his feet dangling out into the open air at the entrance to the mine, a hundred feet above the headwaters of Swartz Creek. He strained, trying to remember what day it was. Pools of water stood everywhere in the mine around him. A steady cascade flowed out of the mine next to him, turning to mist near the bottom of its descent. It disappeared just like I did, Hiram thought, looking down.

He turned to look back inside the mine, irritated at the memory that even the tiniest amounts of running water in the mine echoed loudly all night long, disturbing his sleep. The sound of dripping seemed to grow louder with each passing day. He had tried to predict a rhythm to the water's movement, thinking he could sleep better with noises he knew were coming on a schedule, but he could find no regularity to it. Sitting in the only dry place he could find, he was dangerously close to the ledge at the opening to his damp and perilous prison. Every "lockup" has a name, he thought. I wonder what the other miner called this place, he asked himself?

He had studied the canyon up and down around the mine opening dozens of times, every day since his imprisonment had started: escape was impossible. The mine had been dug in the sidewall fifty feet down from the top and under a slight over-hang in the rock. Unless you knew the mine opening was under the rim it would never be spotted from above, especially from the Horton side of the crevice. Maybe, if someone were in the middle of the rickety old bridge that crossed from the east to the west side above and you waved something and yelled real loud at the same time, Hiram considered, you might be seen and heard.

The late evening shadows already darkened the canyon walls around him, blending with the dark opening to the mine. Every night I disappear again, like a ghost, Hiram thought. "I die again and again," he said aloud. The sound of his own voice startled him. Used to the noisy company of the railroad crew and his family, the silence and isolation was unsettling. Hiram began to worry about his sanity. He forced himself to think again about escape. At least in the thought of escape there was a sense of choice and freedom, he reasoned.

Given Bull's huge frame and the small opening to the mine, Hiram concluded he had never been inside. Several small old shirts and a pair of wet trousers were not anywhere near Bull's clothing size. Hiram examined the pail of water, the ore buckets, and blanket, looking for signs of the owner. After he had examined all the items he had discovered on his first night in the mine, he reached a conclusion.

"Someone has been imprisoned here for some time before me," he said, a thoughtful tone that echoed around him. His voice had a stronger, more confident sound inside the chamber of the mine, he thought. Hiram searched his mind for anyone who had left Bull's crew recently. When he could think of no one, he realized he only knew half the crews: the other half were working up to High Pass from the East side of the grade.

His heart sank in the darkness that loomed every evening, well before sunset. He gazed at the jagged rocks of the creek bottom below and wondered what happened to the man. Had his time of screaming at the canyon walls ended with an insane jump? Hiram knew he could never end his own life that way no matter how desperate his situation became. He gave into imprisonment with one last scream of rage, believing his future had been stolen forever and would now be controlled by Bull Kelly.

Tonight, in the growing darkness and dampness he watched the shadows grow across the canyon wall. Another cold night was coming; it had rained all day and he could hear the creek roaring below him. White, cold, boiling, foaming water now hid the shallow slick boulders he had seen earlier. He shuddered with chills, "Brrr," he said out loud. The creek's noise was almost deafening after a heavy rain.

The sounds echoed up the walls of the canyon, and seemed to come from all directions. Hiram could feel the chill in his bones. He followed the movement of the grotesque, tree-shaped shadows as the setting sun's creations danced along the canyon walls. He let his mind drift, pretending to be moving with them, floating along weightless, upward, and home. He was moving to safety, dancing toward Polly and his girls.

He had filled an extra ore bucket, thinking it would give him more bargaining power, ready for Bull's arrival in the morning. He began to think what else he would ask Bull for, thinking the extra buckets should give him some bargaining power. Hiram examined his worn out pants. His knees were showing, which surprised him. His pants were wet and sagging badly: he was losing weight. He thought to himself, I need better food and more dry clothes or I'm going to die here. Then a thought that nagged at him returned. Had he been there a week? If his memory was correct, he was halfway finished with his imprisonment. Everything depended on Bull Kelly keeping his word. Why would I even think the man would keep his word. He can't free me. I know about the mine and he kidnapped me.

Feeling more like a prisoner again, he took some of the ore in his hands and threw it against the cave wall with a resounding crash, in a rare defiant display. Unable to even see himself in the pitch-blackness of the cave he felt himself to be a fearsome creature capable of anything. Bull had taken everything from him, and the creature was overcome with the desire for revenge. Picking up pieces of the ore he had chipped from the walls, he felt an animal urge to kill, using the sharpest edge he could find among the ore rocks. He began to seethe with thoughts and feelings that were unfamiliar, yet somehow comforting, in the release of his tension.

Drawing in huge gulps of air, he threw another handful of the ore against the wall of the mine in defiance. Then, as quickly as it happened, he was himself again, apologetic at the embarrassing outburst. Suddenly, sinking to new depths of despair he felt himself to be a beggar needing to atone to the world to survive. He apologized to Bull in his mind as well, feeling that he had somehow wronged him. He was suddenly unsure what he had done to bring about his imprisonment. "I'm going crazy!" he roared, his voice echoing up the canyon.

Some of the ore had broken apart from the impact. Many of the sparkling golden flecks of the broken ore pieces were visible in the momentary moonlight. Hiram wanted desperately to find a sharp edge with which to defend himself. He knew the brief silvery moonlight would soon vanish. He began to study bits of the ore. Feeling edges he wanted Bull to feel, smiling at the thought of it, he made slicing movements in the moonlight. Distorted shadows appeared on the walls showing thrusts and lunges at an invisible enemy.

Hiram felt himself relax from the exertion, feeling the familiar fatigue return. He began to wonder if Bull had any of his sample buckets assayed yet. What he saw and felt next made his heart suddenly go wild. Several of the golden flecks appeared to have broken cleanly in two from their impact with the cave wall.

Hiram knew enough about gold to know in its pure form it was soft and pliable. The ore flecks in his hand were hard and rigid. They had broken cleanly from the impact with the mine wall. The flecks certainly looked like gold, but something was wrong with them. He pinched some of the flecks between his fingers. Again the flecks broke cleanly. "My God," Hiram said out aloud. "It's iron pyrite—Fool's Gold."

Hiram jumped to his feet, nearly knocking himself out on the cave ceiling. If Bull discovered the ore was worthless, his life might also be worthless, he reckoned.

Hiram began pacing around the mine like the caged animal he was. He began looking for a way out, like a drowning man, clawing at the walls. He thought about digging hand holds up the face and trying to climb out. His mind began to race from one disastrous alternative to another. He thought about trying to climb back up the thin rope currently tied to one of the ore buckets. That rope, he recalled however, was worn and too flimsy to hold his weight.

Hiram settled on one fact. His only hope was to get the safety harness back down the canyon to the mine. If only he had never taken it off to explore the mine's interior. He tried to picture the pulley system used to lower him down into the mine, but he had no way to reach it. Exhausted, he wrapped himself in the extra clothing and blanket and lay down on the straw, one of the few comforts he had in the nightmare he was living. He felt the jagged rock floor of the mine poking him through the straw. Hiram needed a miracle, and prayed for one.

"Where are you," he roared to God in a voice of desperation?

When he fell asleep, once again he dreamed the same irritating dream: it repeated night after night, tormenting him, offering no rest and no solutions to his imprisonment. It crowded his thoughts during the day as well. Over and over he tried to make sense of it. "More of the devil's work," he finally said out loud. "Not enough for my days to be in this hellhole, but my nights, too."

When he closed his eyes Tuesday night, "she" appeared again. It was a more vivid presence, unlike anything he had experienced before. Hiram was dreaming of Rapunzel, the beautiful maiden imprisoned in a tower in the Brother's Grimm fairy tale. His mother had read the story to him many times as a child. She was a girl with long golden hair. Locked in a tower, she was a prisoner like he was. Both of us need a rescue, Hiram decided. It was the only connection he had made until tonight.

When commanded to, Rapunzel would let down her long braided golden hair for her captor to climb. "I am not your captor, I am not your captor, leave me alone," Hiram repeated over and over. As the last of his consciousness left him in restless sleep, her voice began calling to him. Hiram began to mutter her words, "You are both a captive and the jailer."

She came to him by silvery moonlight. Floating into the cave, she drew near, yet remained just out of his reach. Hiram was suddenly warm from head to toe. Believing in his dream it was Polly, he tried to move closer to her. He could feel her presence, she was reaching out to him. Suddenly, in his dream, she kissed him fully on his lips, surprising him and exciting his passion for Polly at the same time. Electricity coursed through his body, jolting him painfully. Embracing the dream fully for the first time, he groped wildly for her. Feeling a sudden rush of cold water, Hiram woke up, certain that Polly was there, teasing him as she often did, before they were intimate. Hiram looked around the cave. Not finding her, he realized his heart was beating wildly. Something had happened to him, he could feel it.

"There is some comfort here after all," he spoke with relief, anxious to go back to sleep for more of what he had experienced. As Hiram fell back asleep, it was her eyes he could feel on him, looking through him, and the scent of spring Lavender, Polly's favorite.

It came to him just after midnight, waking him instantly. Groping around in the dark, he searched for the clothing left by the previous miner. At last, he knew what the vision was telling him to do to save himself. Around the wet floor of the cave he had everything he needed!

Walking to the mouth of the cave he yelled into the darkness, "The key to this prison door has been in my pocket all along!"

CHAPTER 13

HEALING OLD WOUNDS

Luxury items for personal comfort or entertainment were scarce in these "mill camps." Families that attempted to live "beyond their means," or acquire more than mere necessities, were labeled as "trying to keep up with the Joneses."

–Earl Kelley, from *No Way to R̶u̶n̶ / Build a Railroad*

Wednesday, March 6, 1929

By late afternoon, Gray had finished his evening chores and was restless. He had milked the cow without difficulty, strained the milk through a clean dishcloth and waited impatiently for the last of the sweet-smelling foamy liquid to seep through the porous cloth. After placing two quart jars full to the brim in the pantry on the back porch, he quickly grabbed his coat and headed for the front door.

"You skim the cream off, Gray?" His grandfather asked, noticing his grandson's haste to leave the house. The cream from the fresh milk would rise to the top of the jars within minutes. However, Gray was anxious to get out in the fresh air.

"I'll skim it in the morning before school," he replied. "Unless it's sold already."

"Skim it tomorrow morning then," Verin said sternly, "before you milk again. Chores just add up Gray, when you don't tend to them."

"I know, Grandpa," Gray assured him.

"You going to the store?" Verin inquired. "You better take your hat."

"Just walking," Gray replied. "I might have Mrs. Jack check these stitches while I'm out."

Gray left the cabin and walked toward Horton. The swelling in his face had gone down, but the long row of black cotton sewing thread stitches below his mouth, placed there by Polly Jack in the early morning hours on Sunday, were itching. He wanted to see the Jack women, especially Rosie, and thank them again. He had felt so close to all three of them since his rescue. He walked to the Jack's house and knocked on the door. Rosie had finished her evening chores and came to the door. Smiling, she was clearly glad to see him. As she opened the front door, she produced a welcoming smile, announcing over her shoulder to her mother and sister that they had a visitor.

Gray, feeling the need to announce the reason for his visit, stammered, "Mrs. Jack, will you check them stitches? My grandpa says it's not time for them to come out," he continued. "But, they're itching me to death."

Polly's calming smile made Gray feel at ease. Cradling his injured face between her hands, and inspecting her work, she spoke reassuringly. "My, my," she said. "You are mending."

Tara came bounding from the bedroom at that moment, nearly bowling Gray over with her trademark collision. "Hey, Gray! Come for supper?"

"Naw," Gray said, slightly embarrassed. "Just wanted to say thank you again, mostly."

"Scrub this face with some soap and I'll take them stitches out tomorrow or… the…" Polly stopped speaking and turned away. She left the room suddenly, her face buried in her hands. When Gray glanced at Rosie, her face conveyed the pain he knew the girls had felt every day since their father disappeared.

"We're fixing to leave for Junction City in the morning, need to take care of some…" there was a pause, "…some papers, we'll be back late," Rosie announced with a sniffle. "Tara is going, too. We are riding with one of the Horton brothers; don't know which one," Rosie continued.

"Tara wants you to watch Scout."

"Feed him some orchard grass tomorrow," Tara chimed in.

"Be glad to," Gray replied, turning to Tara.

"Not too much," Tara cautioned.

"We will be back late tomorrow," Polly added, re-entering the room, "if the water level is down at the bridge. With all the rain this week, though, we may be stuck there a while, going to or coming back from Junction City."

Gray was eager to perform this duty, to be of some help to the Jack family. They had saved him and his grandfather. As Gray was walking away from the Jack home, he stopped suddenly when he heard Polly yelling to him, as she stood in her doorway. At first her words made little sense, but then it was clear she was asking about his shirt.

"Gray, where did you get that shirt?"

When he walked back to talk to her, she said, "That's the shirt my husband had on when he left on Monday!"

Gray explained that he had washed what he thought was just an old discard from the dynamite shack. It turned out to be a nice shirt, too big for him, but the flannel material felt soft when he put it on. "Nicer than most of what I have, Mrs. Jack. Guess I wanted to look presentable for my visit. I'm sorry, I'll take if off right now, I didn't know."

"No, Gray, you wear Hiram's shirt," Polly announced. "I think he wouldn't mind, he always wanted a…son to…" she couldn't finish what she was saying and Gray stood waiting. Polly walked over to him and gently touched the sleeve of the flannel shirt that she knew so well. She had washed it a hundred times. She gave him a hug, feeling more of the flannel against her. But, it gave her only momentary comfort.

Her embrace enveloped Gray in a cloud of warmth, bringing his emotions to the surface. She clung to him for only a few moments and when she turned away, back toward the house, Gray wiped a tear from his eye. "I found it in the old dynamite shed," he said. "The one near the Big Bend, close to where you found us."

Not knowing to whom it had belonged to, Gray had inadvertently found a clue to the missing grade master. Turning at the doorway, she spoke to him. "I am so confused!" she said between sobs. "Where would he go without his shirt? Please tell your grandpa about it, he will know what to do."

Gray felt tingly all over and realized he was breathing rapidly. What he had felt and heard here at the home of Polly and the girls had given him a feeling of intense closeness, like he had never felt before. The loss his friends were experiencing was becoming his loss, too. He felt himself becoming determined to help. As he quickly walked back to talk to his grandfather, he wondered if there was still hope of finding Rosie's father alive. One clear thought came to mind as he reached for the latch on the cabin door. Tomorrow, he said to himself, Scout and I will go up the grade and do a search of our own, starting with that shed. School will have to wait. He found his grandfather dozing in his favorite chair. He gently but urgently shook the old man awake to share his plan.

...

Willard Spencer's handshake had but one purpose: he needed Bull Kelly's full attention. He was still irritated after arriving in Horton, by being delayed at the floating log bridge just outside of town. In the mud and rain, he watched the rickety structure rise above the road just as he arrived. After several hours, the water level slowly fell, allowing him passage. Willard was not used to being inconvenienced, either, by Bull's obvious attempts to avoid him. A crushing squeeze of his right hand made the rail superintendent gasp in surprise.

"Have you been avoiding me, Mr. Kelly?" Willard demanded. "I've been here since Saturday looking for you. Didn't the Horton brothers tell you?"

"I've been busy with the search and all…" Bull trailed off.

"I know my visit is earlier than you expected, but I need some answers from you, Mr. Kelly," Willard spoke with great authority. "I have been instructed by the board of investors, of which I am one, to put a salvage value on the whole project unless you can offer gold-plated assurances that you can finish in the next thirty days. I'm told there is no snow along the grade now, so when can I get a ride up to the bunkhouse to begin my audit?"

When Bull tried to look away, Willard suddenly came closer, nose-to-nose with the rail line superintendent.

"Of course, of course," came Bull's smooth reply. "Give me one more week to tidy things up a bit and you can see for yourself how close we are. We are a month to six weeks away," Bull added, testing to see if he had a bargaining position for more time.

Willard's scowl told Bull immediately to rethink his timetable. "We will be laying track right to the top by the end of next week. Then, all twenty men will finish the trestle bridge the following week. I'll work the crews 7 days a week from here on out, if that's what it takes. All the trestle timbers are stacked right here, ready to load, see?" Bull gestured to several large odd shaped piles of trestle timbers and rail lumber nearby bound tightly with metal straps. "It's a shame to scrap the line now when the end is so close. I know money is tight, but the boys deserve a chance to finish what they started," he stated angrily.

"You saw the model," Bull continued. "We know what we're doing here. That just leaves two miles of track down near Bear Creek. It's the Bear

Creek bunch that hasn't kept up their end of the deal. You can't blame me for that mess," Bull pleaded. "My boys can start helping them from this end the following week, when we deliver the rail lumber over the top. All they got is flat grade to finish. We can hold paychecks 'til it turns a profit if we have to. I will make the men understand," he said convincingly, pounding his fist forcefully into his other hand.

"But," Bull said cautiously, "having the track done to the crevice don't get that locomotive over the top, Mr. Spencer. A grade this steep hasn't been done before. We're counting on an engine that hasn't pulled a full load. I realize it's a logger, but I'm still breaking it in. We don't even know if it can be done over wooden rails. I don't even have sand for traction if we start slipping up there near the top."

Willard raised his hand, silencing Bull. "Fine then," Willard said, surprised that a date could be set so easily for a complete inspection. "We spent a bundle on this locomotive; it better work, Kelly."

"A week from Saturday, we'll see the whole completed Horton side of the grade. That's the way it will be, Mr. Kelly," Willard said, prompting Bull. "Right?"

"Of course, of course," Bull replied. "We should be just starting the bridge over the crevice when you come back."

"Oh, and one more thing. Mr. Kelly, are you planning to continue searching for your missing grade master?" Willard asked.

"Going out again in the morning," Bull replied. "It's been a few days. He may have lit out, but the Jack woman doesn't think so. I mostly go for them girls," Bull said smiling, trying to endear himself to Willard Spencer. "It's hard to get the crew interested, so I'll be going on my own tomorrow. That woman bothers me every time I see her," Bull complained.

"Very well, then," Willard said, satisfied. "One more search, then its over," he declared. "You got a railroad to finish. Send her a few…" Willard stopped in mid sentence, thoughtfully choosing his words. "Send her a small stock certificate from the company." Willard Spencer waved a dismissing gesture toward Bull, as if sending a servant away. "Make sure you brag on the company, when you deliver it so everyone knows the A, JC & H Railroad takes care of its families. Brag it up at the mill, too. They need to know the company has a heart, Mr. Kelly," Willard emphasized.

"Mr. Spencer," Bull inquired when the two were backing away from each other. "I can see you are a business man. May I call you Willard?"

"No, you may not, Mr. Kelly!" Willard fired back.

"Too bad we can't be on better terms, Mr. Spencer," Bull replied composed and smiling. "There are…other possibilities here that might interest a business man like yourself. There is something I have withheld from the board until the time is right," Bull admitted. "Something that could lift this line out of the mud, so to speak."

"And what 'possibilities' would you have that I could even think of being interested in, Mr. Kelly," Willard replied, irritated and ready to explode. "If you are holding important information from Mr. Arnold," Willard said angrily, clenching his fists, "he will not be pleased. I will have you fired! That is the business opportunity I have to offer you," a red-faced Willard said, pointing a finger toward Bull's chest.

Willard Spencer was not used to being toyed with and Bull had pushed him to the limit. He was a man with almost full authority, the right hand man of the major investor of the railroad, Joseph Arnold.

"Funny that you should ask for gold-plated assurances, " Bull said as he held up a small leather pouch. Willard snatched the pouch from Bull with a sweeping motion. "What's this?" he scowled at Bull.

"It's another Bohemia Mountain," Bull replied with a silken tone. Willard stared at the pouch, turning his head to the side, clearly annoyed, and not understanding what he held. He was trying to understand what Bull was saying, but his anger clouded his thoughts. Willard realized he was becoming increasingly angry because Bull's composure was remarkable. The man had just been threatened with termination, and yet held his ground.

"Bohemia Mountain, just fifty miles south, has been a miner's paradise until the mines began to play out over the last few years," Bull began.

Suddenly, Willard's eyes opened wide in recognition, as Bull took back the pouch and poured some of the contents into his hand. Willard's mouth dropped open, he appeared faint and stood motionless until Bull took hold of his arm. When Willard started to wobble, Bull gently guided him to sit on a nearby lumber pile. Bull poured the last of the gold ore into Willard's outstretched frozen hand.

Willard didn't speak for several minutes. Finally, looking at Bull, and clearing his throat, he spoke. "Do you have any idea what this means? I think I have underestimated you, Mr. Kelly," Willard stammered.

"Indeed you have, Willard," Bull countered, smiling and feeling he was rapidly gaining the upper hand. Bull was ready to set the hook and knew exactly how to do it. "Is the rumor true that gold will be deregulated and allowed to seek its own value soon?"

"Indeed, the rumor in financial circles is exactly that," Willard replied.

"And what will happen to the value of an ounce of gold if that happens?" Bull asked.

Willard began calculating in his head; he was good with numbers. When he finally spoke, his tone was giddy, yet cold and calculating. "Gold trades now for $22.30 per ounce. It is predicted to double in value immediately, and then the thinking is it will continue to climb as demand grows here in this country. Of course, the President's decision is still pending. The final price could be hundreds of dollars per ounce," Willard concluded.

Bull said nothing, but nodded a knowing and deceitful smile.

"Even a low grade ore lode mine could make us, I mean the A, JC & H Rail line, rich," Willard said.

When it was over, the two shook hands again, this time with gusto. They had made a plan. Willard Spencer departed for Molly's boarding house and dinner, and Bull Kelly to the wigwam burner. Coal was waiting there for his extra pay. Tonight would be his last payday.

Thursday March 7, 1929

Gray woke up early, anxious to put his plan in motion. He had decided to leave Scout behind. When Bull's search party went out today, he would stow away again, jumping off at the first dynamite shed where he had found Hiram Jack's flannel shirt.

In the early morning darkness, Gray walked to the line of cars behind the Gentry and crawled into the tool space beneath the floor of the last car. Nearly falling asleep, he was jolted awake when he felt vibrations through the frame of the car. Bull was starting the locomotive's engine. When only the Gentry began pulling away, leaving him behind, Gray realized Bull had uncoupled the cars from the engine. His heart beat wildly in disappointment and uncertainty.

Thinking quickly, Gray ran to get Tara's pony, Scout. As he did, he realized how determined he had become to see if Bull had been seriously looking for Hiram Jack. He didn't trust Bull and he recalled he had a score to settle from his embarrassment at the Horton Store, the day the Gentry arrived. If Bull was into something, he was going to find out. The Gentry would gain speed slowly until the steam engine warmed to full pressure. Could he catch up? When the locomotive stopped to pick up another man, Gray was already in Scout's saddle and riding hard down the hill toward Horton.

Gray was waiting, hidden in the early morning shadows when the Gentry passed. He watched the engine steam by with Bull at the controls. Gray spit at the locomotive in defiance. Seeing Coal's toothless grin in the cab of the Gentry surprised him. Coal had been recruited it seemed, to help in the search for Hiram Jack. When the logger engine entered the only tunnel along the grade, the whistle blast from the Gentry seemed to last for a full minute. The resounding echo could be heard up to the top of High Pass Crevice.

A different man continued to slumber in the hidden gold mine. The creature looked like Hiram Jack, the dazed Grade Master, tricked and imprisoned there the week before. Bent on revenge and freedom, the creature that would awaken to Bull's calling would not be hungry for breakfast, warm clothing or conversation. The creature would be hungry only for blood.

CHAPTER 14

A Breakfast To Remember

1914
WHEN THE WORLD CHANGED FOREVER

At the turn of the twentieth century,
people were abandoning long held Victorian
values and a new modern world was forming.

In 1914 a shot rang out across Europe that
triggered revolution, innovation and warfare
on a scale never seen before.

VOTES FOR WOMEN

David Hascall

Needless to say, when she got home, she was greatly relieved…that impressionable trip was, as a matter of fact, her very first driving lesson.

–Earl Kelley, from *No Way to ~~Run~~ / Build a Railroad*

Thursday Morning March 7, 1929

Willard had not slept. When he appeared for breakfast, he looked ill and his custom suit was badly wrinkled. The boarding house dining room was full of hungry workers sitting in groups—the regulars. Having arrived to eat before their morning shift, the men knew each other well. The seating area was nearly full and none of the groups offered the railroad big shot a seat. Being ignored in the midst of multiple conversations, clanking dishes and laughter added to Willard's headache as he stood in the middle of the seating area. Searching for a quiet place to sit, his attention was soon drawn to the inviting smells that pulsed from the kitchen each time the swinging pass-through door opened. The mixed aromas from coffee, bacon, potatoes and eggs filled the room in a fragrant cloud of comfort. Willard inhaled deeply, picking through each distinguishable odor, and focused on the one he wanted most of all: coffee. The crash that suddenly came from the kitchen, as several dishes fell to the floor, made him jump.

He recognized several of the work groups that sat together by virtue of their clothing. Several men with black grease-laden boiler suit overalls, with the "Horton Bros. Mill" name on the breast pocket were the first to catch his eye. All three sawyers (saw sharpeners) had chosen to sit with several jitney drivers (lumber carriers). Several timber fallers were also easy to spot from the tall caulk boots stacked near the table, the frayed pant legs and weathered leather epaulet pad laced to each man's shoulder suspenders. The pad cushioned the weight of the heavy falling saws the crews were now using. Willard knew he would never learn their names. Other men he noticed were either gandy dancers from the railroad crew, or powder monkeys (explosive experts). When Molly breezed out of the kitchen she smiled and waved him to the only remaining table.

"Coffee!" Willard yelled as she breezed by giving her attention to one of the tables of hungry men. Annoyed at Molly's lack of immediate response, he seated himself at the small corner table. When Molly finally made her rounds to his table bringing him his much-desired coffee, he insisted, to her surprise, that no one else be seated with him. He opened his briefcase and began poring over several documents. Willard needed to think. He nervously fingered the A, JC & H Railroad stock certificates that he always carried with him, focusing on a small one, worth only $1,000. Funny, he thought, the barely visible train on the certificate doesn't look anything like the Gentry, the new Horton locomotive. Representing the rail line, the certificate was his proof of ownership in case he had trouble making his point with Bull or the Horton brothers.

The coffee was hot and burned his lip, but he hardly noticed. The thought of a gold strike had changed things completely. He would have the sample assayed immediately, of course, to ensure it was gold. After that, he would have a decision to make as to who on the governing board could be trusted with the information. Rumors of instability in the market had persisted for weeks, so maybe there was a way he could use the mine to increase investment. However, if the word got out before there was a substantial return and restoration of the railroad's cash reserves, anxious investors might demand that their stock holdings be converted into gold bullion to hold through the deregulation period. The rumors of an increase in the price of gold would make it a better investment than the railroad. Profit now or profit delayed? Only a fool would continue to wait on the railroad to be completed; it was 4 years over the projected construction time now. Each Shareholder had a legal right to profits and he knew it. Willard frowned, at no one in particular. He had agonized over the dilemma most of the night. "Too many investors," he mumbled.

Maybe it was not the right time to share this information, he thought, nodding to himself.

If the strike was real, perhaps he could secretly buy all the outstanding shares before word got out. He was sure many of the other investors were ready to sell. Confidence in the project was certainly shaken. Rail stocks around the country were being hit hard. As he recalled the dismal showing to investors at Bear Creek, he realized the timing to obtain their shares was perfect. No, he decided, a direct buyout offer was best. However, then he would be risking his own fortune. He could buy as many shares as possible, quietly, through a third party.

Finally, as his cup was nearly empty, it became clear: this was his moment, an opportunity of a lifetime. The profit for the company from the timber receipts, if it ever got going, would be gravy—the long-awaited profits from a prudent investment, for those who had the means to stay with it. If the mine played out as the mines in the Bohemia district had, he could still walk away with a huge profit. Could he collect on both the profits from the mine and the railroad? He needed a plan, and secrecy was essential. He could buy silence from the country bumpkins that sat around him in Horton, he was sure.

The first steps in his plan occurred to him mid-sip, as the coffee ground-laden dregs that clotted the bottom of cup entered his mouth. As he coughed, spewing liquid on the calico tablecloth, ideas began coming in rapid succession. He would give the board a dire assessment of the salvage value of the railroad, then wait for the major stockholders to come to him for advice. He was already planning his presentation to the railroad governing board when Laurie Flanagan entered the boarding house dining room. Once a week, Laurie treated herself to apple pancakes, a local specialty of Molly's. Not finding an open seat at any of the other tables, she noticed Willard's table and marched smartly over to it. She stood quietly with a hand on the back of the open chair, hoping he would notice her. She stood for a full minute, finally getting Willard's attention by clearing her throat. Laurie had hoped for a gentlemanly invitation to sit, and would of course flatter this ruffled but important-looking man. Perhaps she could win his generosity as well. "This coffee is like sawdust!" Willard snarled. "Don't you have some other cup besides this tin piece of trash?" he barked.

"Burn your lip, did you now?" Laurie spoke sympathetically. "Tin cups do that," she added.

"What?" Willard snapped in reply, looking up. He was annoyed that someone he didn't recognize had interrupted his requested solitude. Ignoring her, he returned to his notes.

Laurie began to grow angry at being ignored. When Willard raised his hand, pointing and snapping his fingers, Molly came rushing over. The innkeeper however, had come to greet Laurie and ignored him. The warm greeting between the two women was interrupted by Willard's escalating tirade.

"I asked not to be disturbed," he roared at Molly. Heads turned and several mill workers rose from their seats and stood glaring at Willard. Feeling suddenly the outsider, he began chuckling to the solemn-looking mill workers. "Now boys, nothing here I can't manage. Got two women that both want to sit with me." After an awkward moment of silence, and satisfied by the explanation, the men returned to eating, easing the tension in the room. Soon the sounds of eating utensils on ceramic plates returned.

Everyone relaxed that is, except Laurie and Molly. Willard began whispering to Molly, ignoring Laurie. "Will you ask Miss, what's her name, Miss?" he asked turning briefly to Laurie.

"Laurie Flanagan," Laurie replied.

"Thank you," Willard said, turning back toward Molly. "Will you tell Miss Laurie Flimflam, or whoever she is, that she cannot sit here? I am quite busy, you see."

Molly was shocked. Not wanting to create more disruption for her customers, she looked at Laurie with pleading eyes. Laurie smiled back as Molly retreated to the safety of the kitchen to watch. Willard was about to experience the schoolteacher's Irish temper.

Laurie walked smartly to the counter, picked up a coffee pot and a ceramic cup from a rack on the counter. Not saying a word, she sashayed over to Willard, stood with the pot and waited. His head down, Willard was busy calculating how much of his personal fortune he could invest in the failing railroad. From the corner of his eye he could see the ceramic cup Laurie held in her hand. "That's more like it," he mumbled. When the cup was not immediately filled, Willard waved to his cup in a half-hearted gesture. "Yes, yes fill it up," he motioned, annoyed at having to request the obvious.

Willard's thoughts returned to his work, believing he had made his point with an impetuous woman who now knew her place. His eyes, however, soon became glued to the coffee streaming from the pot, rapidly filling his new cup.

"I find that when coffee is too hot, laddie," Laurie spoke loudly and emphatically, " If I pour some out into a saucer it will cool faster."

"What the Hell you doing?" Willard roared.

As the cup overflowed into the waiting saucer, and onto his stock certificate, Willard jumped up. Fearing the coffee would overflow onto his wrinkled but expensive suit, he stepped back from his chair. Laurie seated herself quickly in his chair and handed the coffee pot to Willard. "Thank you, Mr...Mr..." Laurie solicited Willard to repeat his name.

"Willard Spencer," Willard stammered.

"Now that we are introduced," Laurie gloated, "you may sit down, and yes, I will have some coffee. And, some apple pancakes if you please."

Willard and Laurie sat facing each other. Willard broke the silence. "I've seen your kind before," he said, pointing at Laurie.

"I am a kind person," Laurie replied.

Ignoring her comment, Willard spoke loudly, for all to hear in the dining room.

"You're one of those women that doesn't know her place in a lumber town. Let me guess, next you will pull out your cigarettes and let us all see you can smoke too. You're Flapper trash, you have no business here, go back to the kitchen."

Looking to the room for approval, Willard noticed that everyone stopped eating. No one moved. Eyes locked, Willard and Laurie were doing battle both with and without words.

"I don't smoke Mr. Spencer, but I could if I wanted to," she said calmly. "What was the year, Mr. Spencer, that women got the right to vote in Oregon?"

"I don't give a damn about your right to vote," Willard countered, breaking away from Laurie's gaze. "I came here to help these men and get this railroad finished," he said, gesturing and glancing around the room for support.

Despite Molly's presence in the kitchen doorway, slowly shaking her head at him and a room full of angry faces, Willard pressed on. However, to anyone present, a perceptible defensive tone in his voice was now noticeable. He had begun to realize, somehow, that he had crossed the line by attacking the schoolteacher. Willard was becoming anxious to be done with Laurie and to get out of the confines of the hostile dining room.

"And this is the thanks I get!" he said, standing and throwing his napkin on the table.

"And you would do that how, Mr. Spencer?" Laurie asked in her sincerest voice. "How are you planning to help us?"

"I'm here to help those men there stay working steady," Willard lied. "Everyone here is important to the Horton Railroad. I'm spending my money here too, even though the food is wretched," he scoffed. From the kitchen doorway Molly's mouth dropped open in disappointment.

"Not everyone feels that way, Mr. Spencer," Laurie replied.

"Nonsense!" Willard continued. "These men here have jobs, we take care of people, and no one is ignored."

"You ignored me, Mr. Spencer," Laurie replied. She stood, and walked to the door of the boarding house. Willard gathered his things, the brown stained stock certificate, hat and briefcase, preparing to leave also.

"I meant no disrespect here," he said to the other diners, as he hastily stuffed the soaked certificate into his briefcase. It was one of the loggers who blocked his path to the door.

"Tell the lady here the coffee is the best around or you'll be eating that fancy hat of yours before you leave." Simultaneously, all the workers rose and Willard quickly walked to Molly, who stood with arms crossed glaring at him as he approached.

"Your coffee is...is, fancy," he said, tipping his hat and turning to leave.

"There's no tip on the table, fancy pants," the logger said hoping to provoke Willard to a fight. Willard produced a twenty dollar gold piece and placed it on the table, then quickly walked to the exit door.

Standing in the doorway, Laurie had one final comment. "In that case

Mr. Spencer, since you're here to help, the year was 1912."

"What?" Willard asked.

"The year women got the right to vote in Oregon. And, two years later in 1914, with the start of the war in Europe, the world began to take notice of women. So, when you ignore us I would say you are 15 years behind the time."

Willard stood stunned. Raising his hand to argue, he stopped before speaking and gazed around the room.

Smiling slightly to the crowded boarding house dining room, Willard tipped his hat, squeezed past Laurie and out the door. There were chuckles of laughter still ringing in his ears as he started his company car and slammed it into gear.

CHAPTER 15

DEEDS of DECEPTION

Logging, farming, and construction are the leading most hazardous occupations. Many of the employees were involved in two and sometime three of these high-risk occupations. Yet, amazing as it seems, no one recalls a serious accident or a job related death [in the construction of the railroad], an enviable record for a five-year period, even today.

—Earl Kelley, from *No Way to R̶u̶n̶ / Build a Railroad*

Thursday Morning, at High Pass, March 7, 1929

Waking early, Hiram shivered in the predawn chill. Someone may die today, he thought, as he began making a scarecrow. The previous miner's extra clothing felt wet and stiff as he stuffed both the shirt and trousers with the damp bedding straw from the cave. He mixed in some of the ore to give his straw man some weight. Using his belt, he laced the shirt and pants together by weaving the belt through the bottom buttonhole of the shirt, through a belt loop, then alternating them by lacing through small rips he had made in the tail of the shirt. When he was finished, he realized his scarecrow needed a head and boots. Emptying one of the ore buckets, he opened the collar of the scarecrow's shirt and unbuttoned it part way down. He placed the larger end of the bucket down far enough into the shirt to give the scarecrow a realistic broad-chested appearance and allowed the tapered and narrower bottom of the bucket to protrude up through the neck opening of the shirt. By closing two of the top buttons, he was pleased to see the shirt collar fit snugly around the bucket. Removing the bail from the bucket, he placed his hat on the protruding bucket and fashioned the bail wire to hold the hat in place. Reluctantly he removed his boots and stuffed a straw filled pant leg down into each boot. He removed the bootlaces and cinched the top of the boot tightly, pinching them to the straw man's legs.

Hiram began to review the details of his plan to free himself. He had to convince Bull that he had fallen to his death. First, he would plant the seed of a large nugget too heavy for the bucket to lift without the harness. At just the right time he needed his scarecrow to make a convincing plunge from the mouth of the mine. Bull had to see him fall. Everything depended on the believability of an accidental fall. If Bull believed the mine was empty and he couldn't get the bucket with the big nugget, he might come down to retrieve it himself…and Hiram would be waiting. He knew it was a desperate plan, but he saw no other choice. He tied the ore bucket rope firmly to a large rock in the back of the mine and waited.

He began to second-guess himself and started doubting that his scarecrow would be convincing. At one moment he could feel his confidence building, but the rage that came with it was frightening. Doubts also crept in about his fear of losing control of himself. What if he hit the man harder than he intended, driven by rage and this strange desire for absolute revenge? What if Bull had the other samples assayed and wasn't coming back?

His breathing grew rapid and he became light headed. Calming himself with thoughts of the comforts in his vision, he focused on freedom at any cost. He distracted himself by hefting different size rocks with which to strike Bull. The blow would have to be definite.

He practiced only once on the straw man, realizing what he was about to do would be with him for as long as he lived.

He raised the rock high above his head, bumping his wrist on the ceiling of the cave. Strange, he thought, flexing his hand, I feel no pain. His guided blow picked up speed with dismembering results. The ore bucket head and torso detached and ricocheted to the back of the mine, leaving only half the scarecrow. He had not planned on having to repair the misshaped straw man's upper body. His strength surprised him. He smiled to himself. "Today, I am judge, jury and…" the final word came slowly. At last, gazing upward into the morning sky, "Jacobin."

On their way up the grade, Bull told Coal about the gold mine and how a good deal of ore was already locked away in a shed near the top of the grade. It was theirs for the taking. He bragged up their long partnership in convincing fashion saying Coal had shoveled enough worthless ashes for a lifetime. "It's time to shovel gold!" Coal exclaimed with glee.

Despite feeling like Bull was the best partner he had ever had, Coal asked a question that surprised Bull. "Who's a-mining the ore now?"

Bull gave him a wry smile, but didn't answer. Coal's excitement continued to grow, distracted by thoughts of getting rich and becoming a big shot for the railroad.

Despite news about the mine and the partnership with Bull, Coal had something else he urgently wanted to do while riding the Gentry; something he had been thinking about for days. He wanted to blow the Gentry's whistle in the Big Bend Tunnel on the way back down the grade.

"Yes," Bull finally said. "On the way back you can blow the fuckin' whistle."

Coal stood smiling, watching the trees go by as the Gentry started the climb to High Pass crevice. "Today, I get to be the engineer, a rich one," he told Bull excitedly.

Bull shook his head but said nothing. The Gentry's multi-gear engine needed constant attention on the climb to High Pass. Things changed from day to day along the grade. He made Coal watch out the window on the opposite side for obstacles on the tracks. If there were a tree across again, having his simple-minded partner along would be helpful, Bull reflected. Maybe, if the grade master refused to work, Coal could make a trip down to the mine and convince him otherwise.

Carefully hidden under the seat of the Gentry, Hiram's food was already cold.

CHAPTER 16

STRUGGLE AT THE CREVICE

Access to a hilltop for whatever reason, was achieved by leading a faithful, steady old milk cow to the place you wished to find the easiest ascent. At this place, the cow was fed grain and milked morning and night. Water and hay were in the field at the bottom of the hill. As the cow became familiar with the ritual of eating grain and being milked on the hill, and grazing and watering in the meadow, she would develop a pathway that was the easiest, shortest way up and down, Thereby came the expression, "just a cow path." True enough, the easiest way to traverse the incline.

–Earl Kelley, from *No Way to R̶u̶n̶ / Build a Railroad*

Late morning, Thursday, March 7, 1929

Gray followed the Gentry easily, staying back out of sight. At the end of the completed track he saw the Gentry parked. Bull and Coal were not in view, as they were walking up the unfinished grade toward the summit of High Pass. The air was cold in the early morning chill. Scout nickered impatiently as they began to follow Bull and Coal, climbing the last half-mile to the summit. The going was difficult, as their feet went sliding around boulders, downed trees and stumps that littered the grade, obstacles still needing to be blasted out of the way to complete the last section of track. The pony seemed to anticipate the correct path, however.

Hiram was breathing rapidly, re-thinking every aspect of his plan. At last, the repair to the head and torso of the straw man were completed and he was ready. He waited for Bull to signal him, pounding the worthless ore into his hand to the rhythm of his heartbeat.

When the little bell attached to the bucket rope rang, Hiram knew it was show time.

"Turn loose the bucket," was all he heard from an annoyed Bull announcing his arrival on the edge of the crevice above. It was enough to start his plan in motion.

"It's a big nugget!" Hiram called back up. Coal clapped his hands with glee and began to dance with joy.

"How big?" came Bull's cautious reply, as he grabbed Coal to keep him from falling over the edge of the crevice.

"Took me all day to get it out whole," Hiram countered. "Never seen anything like it. Pull harder and I'll push from down here," Hiram called back, his voice an echo off the canyon walls.

Gray's vantage point was close enough that he could see Bull and Coal staring down into the canyon. The pulley system he saw from his hidden viewpoint seemed important, but gave Gray no clue about what he was about to witness.

Together Bull and Coal pulled on the bucket rope. What they heard next reminded Bull of something he had experienced before in this very spot.

"Oh, God!" they heard Hiram scream. "Help me! I'm falling! AHHHHHhhhhhhh." The scream faded away.

With both Bull and Coal straining at the rope near the edge, they were able to look down into the canyon at the same time. They could see a man falling out of the mine. Coal immediately vomited over the side of the crevice, his hands covering his mouth. He vomited again as he turned away, this time on Bull's shoes. Bull stood transfixed, scratching his chin, watching what he thought was Hiram's body fall toward the swirling current of Swartz Creek, 150 feet below.

"Funny," Bull mumbled, a puzzled look on his face. "It must be further to the bottom than I thought." The body indeed seemed to fall a long time before hitting bottom, but they didn't know it weighed only a fraction of what Hiram weighed.

Hiram retreated to the darkness in the back of the mine and waited. He didn't know if the rock-laden straw scarecrow had convinced Bull that the mine was now unoccupied. He knew that Bull had two choices if he believed Hiram had fallen to his death. Either he would come down to retrieve the bucket himself or he'd find another miner to do the job. Suddenly, Hiram began to lose confidence in his plan, thinking he might have made a big mistake. His worry was short-lived: he heard talking above on the crevice rim although he couldn't understand what was being said. Was it a rescue party? Maybe no one would come down to the mine now if they thought he had fallen to his death.

But he soon had an answer: falling fragments of rock from above meant only one thing: someone was coming down in the harness that he desperately needed.

"Who was it that fallen down thar?" Coal asked, holding his stomach. "How'd he get there Bull?"

"One of the worthless east side bunch," Bull lied. "We were sorta partners, but not like us though," Bull said. "There is some color in the rock wall down there like I told you. Now it belongs to just you and me, Coal, if you want in," Bull urged.

"Seems funny to me, we looking for Hiram Jack, and find some other fella," Coal responded cautiously. "How we gonna fish him out from up here?"

Bull grabbed Coal's shoulders and turned him toward him, forcing Coal to look at him. "Coal, a big gold nugget is down there for the taking, I swear it," Bull said, pronouncing each word slowly. "We'll bring a longer rope and let you down there tomorrow if you want to look for the body. That stupid miner was trouble from the start. Wanted more than half of the diggings," Bull spoke, continuing his lie. "I saw him lose his footing on the slick rocks, same as you, pure accident. He was not as smart as you, Coal."

Bull began to strap himself into the leather harness as he spoke. Then he stopped. "I can't go down there, I'm afraid of heights," he said disappointedly, for Coal's benefit. "I wonder how we're going to get that nugget now?"

Coal considered their problem then finally said, "Partners, you said, right, Bull?"

Together, they examined the harness and Coal agreed it did look strong enough to support his weight and he strapped himself into it. After Bull explained in detail the operation of the pulley system, which Coal didn't understand, Coal became enthusiastic about seeing his new gold mine.

"Don't think you can lift me anyway," Bull said, as Coal was lowered over the side of the crevice to begin his descent to the mine. "It will be your chance to see the big nugget first; it's half yours," Bull reminded him.

"Okay!" Coal spoke enthusiastically, yelling back up toward the rim of the crevice.

Gray left Scout tied to a tree near a clump of alpine grass and moved a few feet closer, his last opportunity to remain hidden, before he would emerge out into the open. Coal was clearly upset by something, but he was too far away to hear what was being said. What was happening? Gray wondered.

"Once you free up the bucket and size up the nugget, I'll pull you up," Bull yelled down.

When Hiram saw a pair of boots come into view at the top of the mine opening, he readied the rock in his hand for use. He knew Bull would need a few moments for his eyes to adjust to the low light in the mine. The bucket rope was tied near the back of the mine. Bull would have to come completely inside to retrieve it. He would be waiting, his barely-containable fury ready to be unleashed. He would get the harness off

Bull and pull himself up to safety. After walking back down the grade, he planned to expose the whole scheme to the Horton brothers.

The blow came out of the darkness and Coal felt nothing. A flash of light and the sound of crunching bone were his last memories before slipping into unconsciousness. Hiram stood over Coal, ready to strike him again if he moved. Looking closer, he realized he did not recognize this man from the railroad crew. Then it came to him: this was the soot-faced clean-up tender from the mill.

The blood pouring from the gash on the man's head was alarming and Hiram, feeling sudden compassion, did his best to stop it. He felt pity and anger toward this man, who was both his enemy and his savior.

Coal began to moan while lying on his back and Hiram wrapped a dirty wet shirt around his head. Unfastening the harness from his limp body, Hiram loosened the ore bucket from the rock and pulled on the rope. Fearing the wrong voice might tip off Bull, he said nothing and waited. He quickly wrapped himself in the leather safety harness.

Hiram felt Coal's face and since it was still warm, he figured the man would survive. He would send someone to retrieve him when he got back to Horton. Hiram spotted a bulge in Coal's pocket and investigated. Discovering Coal's pocketknife, he opened the blade and tucked the knife into his pants pocket. The open blade would be ready when he got to the top of the crevice.

The steady rhythm and strength of the pull on the harness convinced Hiram he was headed home.

"Thank you, sweet lady," he said, speaking softly to Rapunzel. "You are the queen of my dreams."

Hiram glanced upward as he rose to the top of the crevice. His breathing grew rapid; he readied the knife.

Gray, watching from a few feet away, started to understand how the pulley system worked. It had a counterbalance to make pulling things up easier. He had seen his grandpa use a similar device. Something important was happening down in the crevice and he wondered if it involved the missing Hiram Jack. He felt powerless yet fascinated at the same time. He heard Scout nicker behind him, impatient at being left with little grass nearby. Gray turned to make sure the horse was still securely tied to the tree, then looked back to see if Bull had heard the horse. There was wild confusion as a different man emerged part way up and over the ledge of the crevice.

It was difficult for Bull to operate the pulley and watch over the crevice at the same time. He expected Coal to come climbing over the top of the crevice. He was breathing heavily, straining on the rope, ready to yell at Coal at not being more help.

When he saw Hiram Jack's face come into view instead of Coal's, he was suddenly confused. Was this a ghost come to haunt him for causing yet another man's death? Realizing he had been fooled, Bull quickly placed a foot on Hiram's head to keep him from gaining a hold on the top of the crevice ledge. With a violent push, he was able to force Hiram clear of the edge. Hiram swung away from the edge then back, spinning in a complete circle. The two desperate men were only inches apart now as they faced each other. The look on Hiram's face with blood pouring from his nose told Bull the man meant to kill him if he could.

When Hiram swung back toward the crevice wall, dangling in the harness, he swung wildly at Bull. Bull was able to lean back, out of the way easily. Only then did he realize Hiram had extended his reach with Coal's pocketknife: the searing pain in his foot proved that—the knife had punctured the soft leather of his boot… and it remained stuck in place.

Screaming in rage, he jerked his foot back from the edge of the crevice, increasing the damage being done by the knife. Bull quickly let go of the pulley rope and reached for the knife stuck in his foot. Feeling the rope pulley begin to give way, Hiram was desperate for a hand hold on the crevice ledge. The small bucket rope was within reach and he grabbed wildly for it.

"I have had enough!" Bull announced. "See you in Hell!"

Although bleeding profusely and balancing on one foot, he pulled the knife from his boot. He shuddered, realizing the sloshing sound in his boot was his own blood. Fumbling with the slick, blood-covered knife, Bull began to cut the small bucket rope that he believed was Hiram's only remaining lifeline. When the rope frayed and broke, Hiram dropped like a stone, screaming in panic.

As the sudden rush of falling enveloped him, Hiram knew his life was over.

Bull turned away from the crevice, satisfied, but not wanting to see yet another man fall to his death. He needed to get back to Horton before he passed out. Could he explain Coal's disappearance, he wondered? People came and went. However, Coal would be missed. He would make up something for the Horton brothers if he had to. If no one had seen them leave Horton together, he would not have to say anything. He struggled back down the grade to the Gentry, cursing under his breath.

Hiram looked down at Swartz Creek as he fell, its quickly approaching frothy foam awaiting him. He fell right side up, then upside-down, descending end over end. The bucket rope he had reached for was still held tightly in his hand. He did not know why he needed it now. He clutched it, as a child holds a comforting toy even though it no longer offered any hope of survival. He closed his eyes and screamed.

As Bull passed, Gray held his breath and dropped to the ground. His body seemed to be outside his control as he sank deeper into his hiding spot; shocked by what he had witnessed. Should he rush forward and demand to know who Bull was fighting with? Was it Hiram? Was it Coal? An overwhelming sense of powerlessness kept him face down in the mud. The cold took away his urgency to urinate. His instinct to hide for self preservation would satisfy both a sluggish body and an uncertain mind.

"Where are you," Hiram asked his angel, Rapunzel? He seemed to be falling slowly, just as the scarecrow had, as if in a dream. He closed his eyes, wishing for unconsciousness before the impact. The rocks below loomed, and the walls of the crevice blurred as they rushed past. His last thought was of Rapunzel's rope-like golden hair. Pain enveloped him, then calm beyond his understanding. He had misunderstood his dream; this was one final treachery, he believed, at the end of his life.

When Coal awoke, he sat up, wailing at the pain in his head. The echo of his voice floated up the canyon walls. One eye was swollen shut and his mouth, sticky and salty, tasted of blood. A loose tooth dangling by a thread of tissue hung partway down his throat. He gagged and tried to spit it out. The stubborn tooth flopped inside his mouth, like a trapped insect. Locating it and the slender tissue still attached, he pulled on it, screaming again at the pain he caused himself. Someone had hit him, and Bull had got him into this. Squinting out of his remaining good eye through the darkness of the cave toward the opening, a shadow flickered back and forth in front of the cave. It annoyed him, blocking the light intermittently from his remaining eye; it swung back and forth, like an irritating clock pendulum. Holding one hand to his head, he staggered to the opening of the mine. What he saw horrified him.

CHAPTER 17

DEAD MAN DANGLING

David Hascall

What about the wobbling insecure trestles? The solution is simple and inexpensive that had the line been in business any length of time at all someone would have certainly thought of it. Guy lines! Just like we guy power poles, tall communication towers, and in logging operations, the spar tree. Half inch or three-eights cable from the stringers that supported the cross-ties to a stump or tie down.

–Earl Kelley, from *No Way to R̶u̶n̶ / Build a Railroad*

Friday, 4 p.m., March 8, 1929

Hiram swung back and forth on the end of the rope in front of the mine. Suspended upside down by the safety harness, he was unconscious, his legs bound tightly; he appeared to be dead. The rope supporting the safety harness had moved so fast through the pulley when he fell from the top of the crevice, it had jumped off the grooved track. Pinched by the metal bracket holding the pulley from the side, it had slowed his fall, pinching tighter and tighter, until the end of the rope came taut, tied to the stump at the top of the crevice. The slow decent had saved Hiram's life, the bucket rope still clutched in his hand.

"Sum bitch!" Coal spoke aloud. "Serves you right, yer dead," Coal muttered, pointing at Hiram. He spoke to Hiram as if convincing himself that Hiram was dead.

"Bull!" Coal roared up the canyon. "Get me out." Looking again at Hiram, Coal continued his tirade.

"Why'd you hit me?"

Gray felt numb. He knew something horrible had happened, and that Bull was responsible. After Bull limped by, Gray waited and waited, then cautiously approached the crevice and looked over the side. He thought he had heard a voice as he looked down and was shocked to see someone at the end of the rope, hanging there, swinging.

"I'll get help," he croaked, unconvincingly. He turned and ran back to Scout. He jerked up the reins, mounted, and turned the pony down the grade, squeezing his knees against the pony's sides. He had to get down to the bunkhouse and hope someone was there.

When he got close to the Gentry, he heard the locomotive's engine start.

Hiram slowly awoke. He could see Coal's bloodstained face upside down, a blur in front of him. Was he in Hell with a monster? When Hiram moved, Coal was so surprised he jumped back, tripping and falling backward over an ore bucket.

"Sum bitch," Coal screamed again. Frightened, as well as angry that the dead man had moved, Coal retreated to the back of the mine.

Hiram was able to turn over with little effort and realized that somehow the rope harness had saved him. He wiggled his feet, examining the jumble of leather that bound them. With some effort he was able to loosen the leather harness with one hand while holding tightly onto the rope with the other. Soon he was seated in the harness and looking up the fifty feet to the top of the crevice. Hearing a different voice up above—Gray's, and not knowing how long he had been unconscious, Hiram believed a rescue party had arrived. He saw no one on the narrow bridge at the top. Puzzled, he called loudly, his voice echoing off the canyon walls.

"Hello up there, I'm all right—pull me up—two of us down here," There was no reply. The two men now faced each other. Hiram began swinging on the rope back and forth in front of the mine.

Coal broke the silence. "Damn you, give me the harness, I want out of here, no fuckin' nugget, you liar."

Hiram suddenly realized his plea to Rapunzel had been answered. He was in a much better position than Coal, as long as the rope harness held. As he swung by the mine opening a second time, Coal ran forward and attempted to grab the harness rope.

"No nugget, you shit!" Coal yelled again. "Hold still, let me grab you," he said impatiently.

Hiram was regaining his wits rapidly. Pushing off the wall with his feet, his instinct told him to stay out of Coal's grasp.

Hiram looked upward again hoping the harness was tied to something solid and that someone was there.

"There's no gold, Coal, you're the prisoner now, and I got the harness," Hiram reminded him.

"I got the bucket rope," Coal countered. He tried pulling Hiram toward the mouth of the mine using the thin rope.

Hiram held up the end, the frayed strands cut by Bull quite visible. When he dropped it, Coal's eye grew wide and he screamed at Hiram.

"No!"

The free end of the rope drifted slowly down into the Swartz Creek Canyon below, slapping the side of the canyon wall at the bottom of its descent. Both men watched the rope fall and realized it was too short to reach the treacherous stream. The drop from the end of the rope would still be fifty feet or more. The only escape would be upward using the harness.

Coal stood frozen, his anger boiling over again. He spat at Hiram through blood stained teeth. "Go on then, leave me here. Bull will be back," he said.

When Hiram began to climb out of sight, Coal began to change his mind about his hope for rescue. He was finally realizing he was in no position to bargain with this wild man. He had been tricked. Hiram might be able to make it out, leaving him trapped in the mine.

"We can work this out," Coal said, in a conciliatory tone. "Come on in here and lets talk it through. We both want out of here," Coal spoke hopefully. "It's no good, you out there swinging like that," he continued.

Hiram ignored Coal, and continued a slow hand over hand climb to the top of High Pass Crevice. No one would stop him now.

"I'll send you down the harness," Hiram said. "If the rope holds me, I'll send it."

As he climbed, he thought of Rapunzel. Thoughts were flooding his mind again of Polly and his girls. He had to make it out for them. He could hear Coal screaming at him, the sound quickly fading, replaced by his heavy breathing at the strain of his climb to freedom.

As fatigue began to set in, Hiram paused to rest, but his eagerness to reach the top pushed him to climb faster and faster. The cold wind blowing up from the creek below numbed his hands as he climbed; perspiration burned his eyes. But, he climbed on, higher and higher, hooking the rope around one leg with each upward pull, so that he could rest briefly. Soon, though, his rest periods grew longer and longer. Looking up at the old bridge, he saw that no one was there to rescue him.

As he struggled upward, he began to realize his whole life had been about doing things his way. A reputation for hard work is so much a part of who I am, he realized. It would take all his effort to reach the top, he knew—nothing new in that.

He began thinking of Polly. He counted himself lucky to have found a woman like her. He had always assumed she loved him for making their home with his efforts, ignoring his other shortcomings; he had plenty of those. If he made it out, he would make it up to her. Polly had always been there. She inspires me in ways I still don't understand, he thought to himself.

Hiram stopped, his arms and legs screaming at him for relief. He had always got through hard times by recalling pleasant memories. This time, other less comforting thoughts flooded his mind.

He recalled his disappointment at not having a son when Rosie was born. His downtrodden expression had eventually brought on Polly's anger toward him, one of the few times, and he decided he did not want to experience it again. When they were finally able to talk about it, she had said pointedly, "Any child born is a gift, my darling." Did anyone else see it that way, he wondered?

He had decided his farm failed because there were no sons to help him do the work. As he climbed a few more feet it came to him that maybe there was another reason. In the next breath he realized his reasoning about the failure might be incorrect. Maybe the loss of the farm was his fault. There was a new salty taste in his mouth. Hiram's nose began to bleed again.

He climbed on but became alarmed: it seemed like that one particular clump of grass that had somehow sprouted in a crack in the crevice wall, was still in front of him, after many minutes of effort. He was going through the motions but hadn't moved. His clothes clung to him, soaked in sweat. He felt his whole body becoming heavier, like he was wearing a water-soaked blanket. He climbed briefly then stopped and looked upward. I am so close now, he thought to himself. For a moment he became dizzy and felt as if he were underwater. It was quiet and peaceful there, but disorienting. He shook his head, bringing himself back to his task.

"I can't fight anymore," he said out loud. I have been wrong about so many things. It would be so easy to let go, he thought. Maybe Polly would be better off. "I am so cold," he muttered.

Shaking his head again, he climbed on, his teeth clenched, his muscles barely responding. Simple thoughts returned again, ways to end his misery. It would be so easy to let go; the nagging thought came back. Realizing he had already experienced the terror of falling, he climbed another foot. Was it my imagination, my Rapunzel I heard, beckoning me from the top of the crevice, to climb out? What would become of Coal, he wondered, if he let go? Would anyone know he was there? He would be a prisoner like Hiram had been, but forever, in a worthless gold mine. New thoughts of saving this man who had saved him now pushed him upward. Maybe a new start with Polly would be possible.

Bull removed his boot when he got to the cab of the Gentry, while the engine's steam boiler came up to pressure. The knife blow from Hiram had cut through his foot just above his big toe.

How did Hiram get a knife? Bull asked himself. He pulled it out of his pocket and realized it had belonged to Coal. Somehow Hiram had gotten it away from him. The poor devil must have lost the fight. Maybe Hiram had pushed him out of the mine, he considered. No wonder he had such a savage look in his eyes. It would be easier to kill again the second time, Bull admitted, nodding to himself. He shuddered as he recalled the look on Hiram's face, just before he fell.

Bull's foot wound continued to ooze blood and throbbed horribly. His only thought was to get to Horton, and get someone to tend to it. There was no doctor there that he knew of. Maybe, he thought to himself, the Jack woman would clean and dress it: he had been out looking for her husband as far as she knew. He would insist she cooperate before giving her more false information.

It is Friday, he remembered. The crews would need a ride home. His wound would have to be hidden from them on the return to Horton.

It was only when he reflected on the events at the crevice that the fresh horse manure he had seen on the way back down to the Gentry came to mind. Someone else had been near by, undoubtedly watching. If they had seen the fight and someone falling off the crevice ledge, he would need to come up with a story, or maybe something more final. He would find out who it was and deal with them when the time came. Maybe they could be bought with shares of stock in the railroad. He smiled weakly. His partnerships were short lived, it seemed. Bull pushed the throttle of the Gentry forward and started the trip down the grade to the bunkhouse. Then a much broader, knowing smile crept across his face. He had a plan to catch the "snoop."

Gray followed the Gentry cautiously, letting the engine get some distance ahead. When he rounded a bend in the tracks, one of the longer trestles lay ahead. He was startled to see the Gentry sitting squarely in the middle of it, engine running. The cab appeared empty from his vantage point, atop Scout. He dismounted and tied the pony to a tree branch. Where was Bull, he wondered.

"I have to get by," Gray said nervously. Bull may have killed both Hiram and Coal, but the man swinging at the end of the rope might be alive. But why? He realized he would need to explain what he could if the men would listen.

If Bull were nowhere around, he could climb into the cab and move it off the trestle. I can blow the whistle as an alarm, he reasoned. Maybe, Bull had fallen out of the cab and it would be up to him to get the Gentry home, he thought excitedly.

The canyon below the trestle would take time to descend leading the horse. The banks were slippery and the water looked deep. He would have to cross it and climb the other side. His decision to approach the Gentry would satisfy the urgency he felt to save the man dangling below the crevice if he were still alive.

When his hand touched the steep stair railing to the cab of the Gentry, Gray's excitement and sense of purpose grew. He climbed to the cab and slowly slid the door open. A sudden movement from inside the cab startled him.

"You little shit!" Bull yelled.

Gray felt a boot crushing into his chest, knocking the wind from him. Suddenly, he was falling over the side of the trestle, plunging down to the creek below. He saw Bull's sneering grin when he looked upward.

Gray fell into the deepest section of the creek. The cold water sucked his breath away, as he fought to rise to the surface. Bursting out of the water, lungs burning, he coughed violently. He reached wildly for anything nearby. He began crying but couldn't hear himself over the deafening, rushing water. His voice deserted him.

The water swirled and tugged, sucking him downward. He circled, dog paddling, struggling to stay above the surface. Unable to feel the bottom with his feet, Gray began to panic. Arching his back violently he reached upward as high as he could. At the top of his desperate reach, his hand touched the lowest crossbeam of the trestle. Encouraged, he tried again, this time grabbing a firm hold on the rough-cut beam.

He began sliding his hands across the slippery beam. He could feel a sliver of wood puncture his finger, but ignored it. Pulling as much of himself out of the cold water as he could, he worked his way toward shore.

Gasping for breath, Gray dragged himself within a few feet of the bank. He could go no further without giving up his hand hold on the trestle beam. Looking upward, he noticed a ladder attached to the trestle cross members. The construction crew had spent hours installing them on each major trestle, to allow for inspection and maintenance. As he followed the hand holds upward with his eyes, a new sensation swept over him. The trestle was trembling.

Were his hands playing tricks on him? Gray knew he was no longer controlling the shaking in his muscles. He finally realized that a vibrating trestle meant the Gentry was leaving. He was filled with despair. The water suddenly swirled up to his knees. He was losing his grip and his legs were going numb from the cold water.

Gray considered letting go of the trestle and letting the current carry him downstream. The water was always moving and always going downhill; someone would find him. The thoughts escaped as the water began to swirl around his waist. When he could no longer feel his feet, he became terrified he would die. Instinctively, he struggled to hold on to the trestle and realized his only hope was in climbing the trestle ladder.

"I can't climb," he said aloud, protesting his predicament. Gray realized he could no longer feel his fingers or his legs. Losing control of his muscles would mean losing his hand hold, sooner or later. He would hold on until the end, he decided, then let the water take him.

"Always look for a shortcut," Grandpa Verin's voice came to him. But, where is it? I can't find it? Gray thought frantically.

The trestle stopped its trembling sway and Gray knew the Gentry had left. He heard its whistle, likely announcing its arrival at the bunkhouse.

Gray felt everything slowing down and growing quiet. It took precious seconds for thoughts to penetrate the dullness in his brain, brought on by the relentless cold water of Swartz Creek.

The train whistle was a cruel reminder, he thought. The whistle he would never pull. Still, he gritted his teeth as if holding the whistle chord and made a pulling motion downward, one last time, prompted by a vanishing wish to blow the whistle himself. When he lost his grip with one hand, it fell limply to his side. He heard another blast of the train whistle. It startled him from his stupor. Had he actually made it happen, he wondered? His free hand slowly rose out of the water with renewed strength, high above his head, as if controlled by an unseen puppeteer.

He discovered his hand was resting on the next rung of the ladder. Gray began to climb. "Always move ahead, just like a wagon train," he mumbled. His grandpa's voice grew louder as he climbed. Slowly, dragging his numb legs, he reached the next rung.

"Make the best of what you got," Gray repeated over and over.

Chop-flop, chop-flop, the Gentry was moving again, and running fast, heading for home. It faded until he could no longer hear it.

After nightfall, Verin sat rocking is his chair waiting for Gray to return. It had been no use to try to persuade him to give up his notion of searching for Hiram Jack. He recalled how much like his mother Gray was, always taking someone's part. He was more upset about the boy missing school than going out alone. Now, he began to question his reluctant decision to let him go at all. His anger had passed, fading into worry. Gray rarely stayed out after dark. He went down the list of possibilities in his mind. He knew the Jack family were still out of town. With his leg throbbing, his sense of powerlessness grew. He would have to do something soon or trust that Gray could explain his late absence when he returned. He began to wonder if his grandson had been thrown from the horse somewhere along the grade. When he exhausted the list possible disastrous alternatives, he began to make a list of more hopeful ones. The list was short and soon the rocking chair ceased its motion and Verin fell asleep. His grandson was good in the woods and was nearly grown after all.

CHAPTER 18

BIGGER INVESTMENTS;
GREATER EXPECTATIONS

But this first section was the easy part. As ties and tracks were laid, the "Loco" brought supplies and materials right up to the construction site. In building, this is a critical factor that determines whether or not a project is expedient, efficient and successful.

—Earl Kelley, from *No Way to ~~Run~~ / Build a Railroad*

Late Friday, March 8, 1929

Rosie sat looking nervously outside. Arriving late from Junction City, she had expected to pick up her homework and hurry home, but she had been asked to stay after class and was uncertain why. Tara had laughed at her, assuming she was being punished for misbehavior.

"Shame, shame," Tara teased, pointing an index finger at Rosie and rubbing her other index finger across it. "I'm gonna tell mom."

"Pay no attention," Laurie whispered. Seeing Rosie glancing nervously again toward the door, Laurie knew her first lesson would be a short one.

"Please listen carefully," Laurie told Rosie. The door opened suddenly. Instead of Tara, it was Polly who entered, walked over and stood behind Rosie. Laurie nodded politely to Polly, who remained standing, looking annoyed and fearful.

"I need my Rosie at home, right now," she said. "She came to pick up her school work from today. Has she done something?" Polly asked. "I'm here to straighten it out and get her home."

Laurie looked into Polly's eyes, searching her, surprised at her suspicious nature. After a long pause, feeling uncomfortable with Laurie's gaze and silence, Polly looked away.

Regaining her composure, Polly took a deep breath and said. "Well? My girls both have chores after school. We just got home from Junction City and our horse is out, likely jumped the fence. And, you know my man is missing a week, likely not coming home to help. We have to make some… changes now…" she said her voice trailing off. "We were just barely getting by before, now I don't know. They don't hire any women at the mill and I need both my girls to look for the horse and Rosie helps me sew in the evening. We make napkins for the boarding house now. We just want to be left alone. Come along Rosie," Polly said, pulling Rosie to her feet.

Laurie moved her chair close to Rosie. "There is something special about you," Laurie began, ignoring Polly. Her attention fully focused on Rosie, she continued. "I have noticed it, and I want to help you discover what it is."

"Yes, yes, I want to know what it is!" Rosie answered excitedly, giving a hopeful glance at her mother.

"Tomorrow I would like you to tell me the number of books you have at home, what they are about, and how many of them you have read," Laurie said. "This is a different assignment from schoolwork because it's not graded. That is all, good night, Rosie," Laurie said with a smile.

"My Rosie is just fine already, she'll not be staying late again," Polly said, angry that her earlier request to be left alone would likely be ignored.

"Why don't I come by your home then, after school, say on Tuesday, Polly?" Laurie asked. "If that would be more convenient. We can trade services. I won't be any help for a while, with the sewing I mean, you can teach me how to stitch so I can help. I'll give Rosie extra lessons that way, and can see both of you. My extra lessons are very short, I assure you," Laurie said expectantly. "There are great women I want to tell Rosie about. Maybe we can all be better friends."

"Can she, Mama? Can she?" Rosie pleaded.

"We'll see," Polly said, "We'll see."

As Laurie opened the outer door of the school to let Polly and Rosie out, Polly stopped in the doorway. Turning slowly, she spoke. "I know you mean well, and all. I did want to thank you for coming last Sunday," Polly continued. "I felt so alone."

"If Tuesday is too soon for another lesson for Rosie, we can put it off further. I know this is a difficult time," Laurie suggested.

"A longer delay won't be necessary," Polly said, remembering the kindnesses she had been given. "Would you like to come to supper some day soon also, Laurie? I do want to thank you in my way but it's so hard to visit out right now. Tomorrow is the service for Hiram; I don't expect to entertain much…" Polly said sadly, her voice trailing off.

"Lets wait and see how you feel after that then," Laurie said, with a sympathetic expression.

…

The Keys brothers, twin pastors in the Pilgrim Harvest Church, arrived late on Friday, March 8. Preacher Earl was the twin that always seemed to take the lead when it was required. He was driving a borrowed car when they attempted to cross the floating log bridge over Lake Creek. The car pitched wildly then rolled from side to side. As the log bridge had not quite aligned with the road, and brother Earl was unfamiliar with the crossing technique, the car bucked and jumped and nearly went over the side into the fast moving steam. It was preacher Mearl that shrieked, "this is not the river Jordon, slow down my brother, I don't need another baptism!" Both brothers were shaking badly when the crossing was over, feeling like they had descended deeper into uncharted territory. They had not expected to officiate at a funeral the same day as the scheduled church revival in Horton. However, funerals meant a rare opportunity, as most of the town would be in attendance. It would be an excellent launch of their church-planting season.

The twins' aspirations of rising to director level of the Western Region of the loosely affiliated Pilgrim Harvest churches might hinge on a solid performance in little towns such as Horton, they had quickly decided. What would make an impression on the other church leaders would be increasing the numbers of new churches. As the Horton church was unlikely to be rebuilt any time soon, following a fire the previous year, they would certainly get the credit for re-planting the church. Peter Horton, who greeted them at the floating log bridge, told them that the schoolhouse was the only available location for both the funeral and the church revival service. He had little information about Hiram Jack as he primarily ran the family lumber sales business in Junction City.

After settling the twins at Molly's boarding house, he referred them to the proprietor at the Horton Store for information about Hiram and the Horton community church.

"Good man," the store owner said. "Pays his bills, works hard, nice family, too. Got a couple of girls. One of um is a real live-wire. Family lives on the hillside here behind the creek," he continued pointing with his head, up toward Hiram's company home. "Shame he disappeared, just when the railroad is about to open for business. Been a long time coming. Seems kinda of a funny-business, no one seems to know much. Not like him at all, to disappear like that." At that, the store owner turned away, shaking his head sadly and returned to his business of stocking shelves. "Oh," he said, "one more thing." While the twins waited the man gathered an enormous chaw, bent over and spit it perfectly into a small brass spittoon. "Folks here take care of their own. We don't ask for much from outsiders. Being you're men of the cloth and here to give the man a proper send-off, your credit is good here. Horton brothers are covering your needs while you're in their town."

Laurie had eagerly agreed to offer her room at the school for Hiram's funeral service. Although less eager to have the church revival service there as well, she reluctantly gave in to Mildred and Andrew Horton, chairman of the school board.

...

Willard Spencer had driven to Portland with his ore sample carefully hidden in his briefcase. He still had a dilemma. He debated if he should tell his boss, Joseph Arnold, anything. Telling him about the gold strike before the lode was confirmed did not make sense. He would be giving away any advantage in the matter, he was sure. Arnold owned fifty one percent of the A, JC & H project. The arrogant bastard had already made his money, Willard reasoned. He also had his name on the railroad, what more did he need?

"A for absent," Willard muttered aloud, nodding to himself. "I hardly ever see the man." He decided he would keep Joseph Arnold in the dark, for now. The less all the investors knew, the better, he decided. The remainder of the interest in the Horton project was spread among a few Portland investors, the Horton brothers and their mill, the people of the Lake Creek Valley and himself. Many of the folks who owned property along the grade had eagerly exchanged it for stock, a significant boost to the cash flow problems that had occurred at the start of the grade building.

Arnold had been afraid of government involvement with his railroad. Most of the big time investors quickly lost interest for that reason, Willard recalled. His task over the last several years had been holding the existing investment group together, and keeping the government out of their business. Willard would plan to buy all outstanding shares he could if the gold strike was real, his second secret from Arnold.

In the beginning, capital was slow to come in, Willard recalled, until Arnold had peddled his converted railroad truck engine invention door-to-door. All we had to do was offer some stock for passing through their miserable patches of timber. A homegrown project totally free of oversight by any government agencies held the ultimate appeal, they had decided together. It had been the motivation for both of them in their extensive involvement. As long as the money kept coming in, everyone got paid and everyone was happy.

Willard knew Arnold had made plenty of money through re-investing the thousands of dollars that came in, while spending very little on the railroad. He had watched the dollars flow in and out of his accounts in Portland and Eugene. Arnold could walk away. Willard Spencer did not see how he, himself, could. His shares would either need to be sold for a fraction of their value, if they could be sold, or made into something gold-plated. The later alternative had become his only choice.

He wondered why he had lost so much sleep over the last few days. It was a simple solution—assay the gold—buy secrecy from Bull and anyone who finds out, and move the gold by rail to Bear Creek when the line was finished. The log station and planer mill be damned; he didn't need them. What he did need, however, was to keep all the crews working full speed from both Horton and Bear Creek. A thousand more dollars invested in wood and wages would be the best investment he would ever make while things got sorted out. In these changing economic times there were few good investments in this part of the country.

Arnold would be pleased, if—and when—he found out. Gold was timeless, and surprising wealth would make forgiveness easy. But, Willard decided, he would keep the secret from him as long as possible. When Arnold did find out, perhaps a sizable amount of ore would already be turned to cash and safely deposited somewhere else solely in his name. I have always wanted to live in San Francisco, Willard thought. They were building a new zoo there, and a spectacular bridge across the golden straights at the entrance to the San Francisco harbor. "A golden invitation," Willard said out loud, a sly smile spreading across his face. In order to continue the charade with Joseph Arnold, he would do what ever it took to keep the secret.

When Willard reached his office, strangely, Arnold's whereabouts were unknown to his secretary and he was unable to report on his inspection of the railroad in person.

He has already lit out, Willard concluded, nodding to himself, as he stood outside the office. He decided to write a letter to his boss instead.

Friday March 8, 1929

Dear Joseph,

Following my on-site evaluation of the west end of the A, JC & H railroad project, I am pleased to report that the Horton sections with be finished within ten days. It is my estimation that we will be finished with the project within thirty days. I see no reason at this time to anticipate a salvage sale of the line and its equipment. The market for both timber and finished building grade lumber has never been stronger, and I anticipate robust markets in both the Willamette Valley and elsewhere.

> *Sincerely,*
> *Willard Spencer Jr.*

Quickly rushing to the bank, Willard gambled that Joseph Arnold had left for parts unknown. He withdrew the final one thousand dollars left in the railroad payroll account. This would not be that unusual given the ongoing needs of the project. He would put up any additional money himself, if needed. Keeping all the crews working from both ends of the grade was more important now than ever before and easily explainable if Arnold reappeared. Willard knew he would need a way to get large amounts of ore exposed from the hard rock mine. If the assay were good, he would visit a heavy equipment company in Eugene. A steam-powered shovel could be shipped to Horton and make quick work of the remaining grade and get on to the real business; exposing the gold bearing ore.

CHAPTER 19

A SERVICE TO REMEMBER

Should one tell a lie which does not hurt you nor anyone else,
why not say in your heart that the house of his facts
is too small for his fancies, and he had to leave it for larger space?
–Kahlil Gibran, from *Sand and Foam*, 1926

Saturday, March 9, 1929

Verin awoke with a start. "You here, Gray?" When there was no reply he staggered to his feet and limped to Gray's bed to see for himself. Not finding Gray in the cabin he began shaking with fear. "That boy means everything…" he said out loud. As he milked his Jersey cow his fear began to preoccupy his thoughts. He would find help for a search at the funeral as the Horton brothers and the railroad crew would be there.

The twin pastors, Earl and Meral Keys were surprised that they had not been able to gather information about Hiram's mysterious disappearance at the boarding house or the Horton store. Both paced nervously in front of the school. "Do we have a death here or something else," Earl lamented? "There is no body to bury," Mearl added. "This tight-lipped community might prove to be a 'tough nut to crack,'" Earl concluded. When people began arriving for his funeral service, the brothers stood on opposite sides of the entry, just outside the schoolhouse door. They knew a personal handshake was always a good touch for a funeral as well as their ministry. They asked polite questions about Hiram, anxious to learn anything they could.

"The family appreciate your coming," preacher Earl said repeatedly. "Are you a friend or part of the family of the deceased?"

His brother, preacher Mearl, quickly scribbled notes of information he heard from his brother's questions. Over and over the script was repeated until, arriving late, Polly Jack and the girls appeared.

When Preacher Mearl, on a rare miscue, mistakenly greeted Polly incorrectly, as if she were a simple funeral attendee, she stood in stunned silence and did not extend her hand. Preacher Earl broke the silence.

"Mrs. Jack?" When Polly nodded, Preacher Earl continued. "Please follow me."

With the girls tagging behind, they made their way inside toward the front of the room. When they passed Laurie Flanagan sitting along one aisle, Polly extended her hand in greeting. Laurie gave her hand a brief squeeze as the group passed by.

One last person came into the school classroom—turned sanctuary— and sat in the back. It would be Joseph Arnold's last visit to Horton. Unsure how he would be received with the dire news of the railroad's future, the heavily-bearded railroad tycoon sat unnoticed.

"Let us begin with a word of prayer," Preacher Earl spoke as he gestured for all to rise. When the assembly was seated again, the hastily assembled service began with a reading of the 23rd Psalm. Then the floor was opened to anyone who wanted to speak on behalf of the deceased.

Both the Keys brothers began listening carefully. Any facts they heard now could be useful and woven into the church-planting revival to follow. Information about these people in this out-of-the-way place was desperately needed.

Andrew Horton stood and spoke on behalf of the combined mill and railroad company. Several of Hiram's co-workers told humorous stories about him. There was polite laughter from the crowd.

Verin Palmer limped forward and talked about Hiram as a pioneer and master builder who left a lasting legacy of accomplishments. When no one else stood to come forward, an awkward silence followed.

Polly stood and spoke. "Hiram, wherever you are, I love you. I am sorry we could not continue our journey together, or finish the dream you had about our community railroad. If the Lord has taken you from me, then he will bring us back together someday." She seemed unwilling to speak further and returned to her seat.

A girl carrying a flute appeared at the back door and was immediately waved to the front. The Keys brothers were both sweating profusely.

The girl struggled through Igor Stravinsky's Octet. Just as the music ended, Preacher Mearl noticed from his vantage point at the back of the room that his twin now had both arms extended toward the high ceiling of the classroom. This pose was highly unusual. When his brother Earl dropped to his knees at the front of the service, Mearl rushed forward. To his surprise, his brother began to speak.

"There is trouble in the House of Horton," he shouted. "The Lord has spoken in this place, and there is trouble!"

Preacher Mearl's eyes opened wide and his mouth dropped open. He had never heard his twin brother speak this way. It had never been part of their funeral script before. Preacher Earl began to sway back and forth, his arms following his body as if blown by a heavenly breeze.

"The Lord God has heard our cry. Hiram Jack will be found!" Preacher Earl exclaimed in a thundering voice. The assembled crowd collectively gasped! Preacher Earl's eyes glazed over, and his head dropped to his chest. He looked exhausted and ready to fall the rest of the way to the floor. Polly put her hand over her mouth and was immediately encircled by her daughters and other people seated nearby.

Preacher Mearl was dumbfounded, and stood holding his brother upright to keep him from falling forward. Around him, mouths opened wide as the Horton townspeople looked at each other, stunned. Had they just heard a prophetic utterance? As if on cue, everyone stood.

The flautist, feeling compelled to play another song, began the only other song she knew by heart, "Onward Christian Soldiers." The hymn by Anglican priest Sabine Baring-Gould was well-known. Those that knew the words began singing, some marching in place.

Escorting his brother to the back of the room, Preacher Mearl no longer knew what to do. The service would now be up to him to finish. People were watching, waiting for him to say or do something.

All at once, without a word, people began moving down the aisle and gathering around the twin preachers. Everyone was talking at once and wanted to touch Brother Earl. Mearl heard multiple offerings of support for their ministry. Hands stretched forward. The offering plate the twins had set on a chair by the door began to fill quickly, with even several stock certificates in the A, JC & H Railroad appearing in the plate. Preacher Mearl was astonished. When the first members of the congregation exited the school, those inside heard shouting from outside.

Rushing to the door of the school, Polly pushed past friends and neighbors who were frozen in place. Holding onto the empty flagpole for support was her husband, Hiram Jack. Sitting close by on the ground holding an old shirt to his head was Toby Coalanski. Next to him, shivering with cold, sat Gray Palmer. Mildred Persons promptly fainted into the waiting arms of Andrew Horton. Verin and Polly reached the schoolhouse door at the same time, each waiting for the other to exit. Hiram and Gray were soon encircled in loving arms. Unable to reach her father in the frenzy, Tara ran to Scout who was feeding nearby on some grass. Despite her prolonged hug around the horse's neck, Scout seemed unimpressed by all the commotion.

CHAPTER 20

NEW BEGINNINGS

No one living today from that era seems to believe the railroad was ever intended to go past the Southern Pacific track at Bear Creek and on into Junction City. Nor was the original intent for hauling logs. The original concept was to haul the rough sawn lumber from the mill in Horton to a resurfacing planer mill at the Bear Creek terminal and ship via the Southern Pacific Railroad.

–Earl Kelley, from *No Way to ~~Run~~ / Build a Railroad*

Sunday, March 10, 1929

Their night had been filled with warm cuddling and comforting lovemaking, unlike anything either one of them had ever experienced. Smiling with contentment, Polly's thoughts came in excited bursts as she stirred awake. It was clear her husband regarded her differently. He had been gentle, unhurried in their lovemaking, responding to her needs above his own; one of the few times in their marriage she could recall this ever happening. When they came together, she felt a closeness she had longed for since their wedding night. They reached a climax at the same moment for the first time. As she began to awaken, her head swimming from the smell of their lovemaking, she still lay snuggled next to him, breathing in his ear, her naked breasts available and anxious for his touch. She had fallen asleep nearly on top of him, yet felt fully rested. Maybe things will be better now, she thought. Hiram had been sleeping heavily, but after being tickled by Polly, he began to awaken. Several yawns were followed by a sudden grab for her that surprised her and made her squeal with delight. A long embrace followed; he was in no hurry.

As they began to waken, suddenly the quiet morning was interrupted by voices at their front door. They were startled back to a more painful world.

"Hiram, you awake? We need to talk about Bull!" It was the voice of Verin Palmer, who stood outside with Gray, Andrew Horton, and Coal.

Collecting his thoughts, and making a sad face at Polly at being interrupted, he got up and sat on the side of the bed, pulling on his clothes. As he pulled on his boots he called to the men waiting in the cold outside. "I think I stuck him in the foot with Coal's knife. Things happened so fast up there. I'll be right out..."

Polly quickly retreated to the girls bedroom where they still slept quietly, putting on her dressing gown and coat.

"We need to tend to Bull," Verin said in an ominous voice. "He's done plenty wrong, and we need some answers. There is blood in the cab of the Gentry too; he may need mending. Mrs. Jack, can you come along, too?" Verin asked.

Hiram replied, "We'll both step outside in just a minute..."

They stepped outside onto the front porch, and Andrew Horton added, "It might be a good time to find out why he done all this wrong to these men. My brothers and I intend to make things right to you folks."

Gray felt as if he was a foot taller being included as, "one of the men."

"Gray has quite a story about what he saw at the crevice," Verin said. "The madman nearly killed him on one of the trestles on the way back down the grade," he continued angrily. "Darndest thing I ever heard too: Coal here says your pony was still waiting for him to fetch it home, tied to a tree up by the trestle, the whole time. I'd like to give that horse a good slug of grain."

"And, we need to know about what happened after that," Andrew added. "None of Bull's crew has heard from him."

"Your boy is lucky to be alive, Verin," Hiram answered. "Coal and I found him laying on the tracks above the Big Bend. He could hardly speak, being soaking wet, and half-dead from the cold. He said Bull kicked him off the Gentry, for no good reason."

"I mean to get a lot of questions answered," Verin barked, pounding his fist into the palm of his hand.

"No one has seen Bull anywhere since the Gentry come home yesterday," Andrew said. "With what he done, he may have left town."

The group trudged over to Bull's company house and Coal knocked on the door. He had not told the group anything about his part in the partnership with Bull in the gold mine, saying only that Bull had forced him to check out the hole in the rocks, then left him, like Hiram, to be a prisoner. There was no response from inside the house.

"Bull, you in there?" Coal shouted. "We need to talk." He spoke again, playing his part as another one of Bull's victims. "Why'd you leave me up thar, at that damn crevice?" Again there was no answer.

The door was unlatched and the group entered, Verin in the lead. All the company houses were twenty by twenty feet square, so Bull was easy to find. The first thing everyone noticed was the horrible stench coming from the back of the house. Sliding aside the curtain that separated the sleeping room, the group could see Bull slumped in a chair beside his bed. Still dressed in his company boiler suit, his foot elevated on the bed, Bull looked feverish and seemed somewhat delirious.

"What the fuck you doing?" he mumbled. Surprised anyone would barge into his home uninvited, Bull tried to stand. "Get out!" he said weakly.

In his feeble and barely-conscious state, Bull raised his arm over his head as if expecting a blow to come. When he tried again to stand, Hiram put his hand on his shoulder and sat him back down. Bull dropped into his chair.

"You?" Bull gasped in surprise, looking up at Hiram, his head dropping to his chest.

"We supposed to be partnas, you fuck," Coal said, looking to the others for confirmation. "Pardon, Mrs. Jack," Coal apologized, turning to Polly nearby.

Polly knelt down, her dispassionate but focused gaze locked on Bull's foot. Grimacing from the smell, she set her jaw and gently removed his boot and blood-soaked sock, despite his moaning objections. Bull's foot had turned blue and several toes were black. It was clear the disgusting smell was coming from Bull's injury.

"My, my, Mr. Kelly," she said. "You need mending. Your foot has the fever; you might lose it."

"My foot…?" Bull mumbled. "Not my foot," he choked. "Got to keep my foot to spend my…my gold," Bull sputtered. The group looked at each other and shook their heads. Gray hurriedly walked outside and threw up his breakfast.

"Talk about your foot later," Verin said. "Give us some answers, and we'll let Mrs. Jack, here, tend to you. Maybe she can keep you from dying."

"Gold or no gold, why you treat these men so bad?" Verin asked, shaking Bull as he began to slip to unconsciousness. "They work for the company and they work hard," he continued angrily.

"It's fool's gold in the crevice, you cold-hearted bastard!" Hiram shouted. "It breaks in your hands," gesturing a breaking motion. Hiram removed several ore chunks from his pocket and thrust them in front of Bull's face, jostling him again to keep him from nodding off. "How many men you tricked to do your mining?" he demanded.

Bull pushed Hiram's hand away defiantly. "You no fuckin' expert," Bull muttered. "Not all of it's bad. Better hope it's gold. If there is no gold, then there is no company," Bull declared. "The line is broke. Company knows. Their man Spencer is getting the assay, may be enough color to finish the line. Horton Brothers don't know shit! Keep the secret, you people; we'll all be rich. Help me out here, I meant no harm." Having said that, Bull passed out.

The men looked at each other in surprise. No one said anything until Polly broke the silence. "We need to get him on the bed," she said, speaking with authority. "I need some hot water. Gray can you tend to that?"

Coal, Verin, and Hiram moved Bull to his bed and propped his leg up on a pillow, so Polly could begin cleaning Bull's wound.

Andrew was anxious to leave Bull's house to find his brothers. "The railroad investors knew about this, and let it go on, not telling us?" Andrew said incredulously. "My brothers will be making a trip to Portland with fire in their eyes. They meant to cut us out!"

Verin had calmed himself and had become suspicious… "You ARE the company," he said, looking at Andrew and grabbing his arm—preventing him from leaving. "You sure you didn't know about the gold strike?"

"We are honest lumber men, not miners," Andrew said defensively.

"Easy there; let's not fight amongst ourselves. If there is gold in Spencer's sample, miners will move right up here from Bohemia," Polly suggested. "That will be the real problem."

"Polly's right," Hiram said thoughtfully, giving his wife's shoulder an approving squeeze. "We got bigger problems to worry about. Sooner or later the word will get out and our little town will be run over by desperate men."

"Land owners and miners both will be staking claims, blocking the tracks," Coal added, surprising the group with his rare insight. "Claim jumpers, too."

"We'll be lucky to get the Gentry through to the mine," Andrew reckoned.

"Won't be a secret for long," Verin said, as the group watched Polly do her best to clean the wound in Bull's foot.

"How are we going to keep a whole town quiet," Polly asked, turning to the men watching over her shoulder?

"We'll have the same mess here they got down Bohemia way," Hiram added, shaking his head.

Gray built a fire in Bull's stove and put a kettle on to heat. Within a few minutes the pot of warm water was brought to Polly and she began her work in earnest. Gray, having rejoined the men and feeling the need to contribute said, "We could just keep that floating bridge too high for travel, like a drawbridge." There was a chuckle from the group as they watched Polly cleaning Bull's wound. Each man seemed to feel the discomfort with his own grimace each time Bull winced in pain. Gray began rubbing his chin, remembering his own experience and Polly's gentle touch.

Finally to lighten the mood his grandfather said, "We're trying to open this country our way with the railroad, not close it, Gray," a wide smile on his face.

Coal was conflicted. If he stayed on helping Bull, he might be accused of participating in the kidnapping of Hiram. He had let slip that they were partners. However, going with the others meant charting a new course of respectability. Finally, he sighed deeply: his future clearly meant changing sides.

Once the wound had been cleaned as best as Polly could, the small group departed, leaving Bull there on his bed to rest. Coal reluctantly agreed to look in on him the next day.

CHAPTER 21

BONDS AND BOUNDARIES

David Hascall   The Longest Wooden Railroad

Ernie Smyth somewhat vaguely recalls what he believes to be the only mechanized equipment used in the excavation and grading of the railroad bed. He is under the impression that towards the end of the project they brought in a steam scoop shovel for some of the excavation on the summit. There are, in fact, several cuts in excess of thirty feet or more in height along the ridges on the summit. These would seem to substantiate his belief.

–Earl Kelley, from *No Way to ~~Run~~ / Build a Railroad*

Early Monday Morning, March 11, 1929

Willard Spencer had paced back and forth in front of the assay office in Portland, and when it opened at 9:00 A.M., he presented the clerk with the ore sample and began the tedious process of registering a new claim. He gave a fictitious location for his gold mine. When the clerk reported that it was highly unusual to have a man dressed as Mr. Spencer delivering a sample of ore, Willard grinned. The smile on his face was replaced with a frown when he was informed that the assay could not be finalized until the following day. The agent said it looked like flour gold and pyrite mixed in his ore sample, which sounded hopeful. The key would be how much of each.

Early Tuesday Morning, March 12,1929

Having spent the previous evening contacting his Portland investors, Willard was pleased with his work. All of them were anxious to unload their portfolios of the failing railroad's stock. He now owned thirty-two percent. Although not equal to Arnold's fifty-one percent, Willard's confidence was growing. He would take charge of the completion of the last section of track and planned to enlist Bull to keep everyone quiet and away from the mine.

Willard's hope was to keep reducing the number of investors. The ownership would thus be between him, the Horton brothers, Arnold, and a mix of local folks in the Lake Creek Valley. Four shareholding groups were still too many, though, he had decided. If the gold strike were genuine, he would find a way to cut out the Horton brothers, the largest investor group next to himself and Arnold. It all depended on the assay results. He was sure the people of Horton and the Lake Creek Valley would sell their shares as well, if the price was right.

Willard, unaccustomed to waiting for anything or anyone, burst into the assay office the moment the door was unlocked. The surprised clerk still had his hand on the door knob, and jumped back in surprise. Willard's hand trembled slightly as he opened the official looking report, stamped in large letters "ASSAY." He took a deep breath and read. When he finished, however, he frowned impatiently, unclear what the results meant. Taking the clerk aside, he got the information he needed: his ore sample had an estimated gold yield of 10 g/t AU and was a very positive ore sample. He had a gold mine! Willard clapped his hands together in excitement.

With his heart in his throat, Willard listened impatiently while the agent began schooling him in several very specific lode-mine requirements in an area with congested mining activity. In the midst of the information about restriction in tunnel length, he simply turned and left, leaving the agent dumbfounded. Once he understood that gold ore was measured in content per ton of aggregate he had but one remaining objective while in Portland. For a brief moment he had changed his mind and planned to share everything with his boss, Joseph Arnold.

He went as quickly as he could to Arnold's office. The door was locked and through the glass pane in the door he could see half-empty boxes lying on the floor. One sign on the door was a forwarding address, his, at the Eugene Hotel. The other was a note addressed to him. Willard opened the note and read:

Dear Willard,

As you can see, the office is closed. By now, you have undoubtedly determined the salvage value of our railroad. You have been a good and loyal employee. The failure of the Bear Creek station to demonstrate the value of our project to new investors was the end, as far as I can see it. I am surprised however, that you did not report this to me in person. Thankfully, your superintendent did. However, I don't trust him.

Please salvage what you can and call it a final payment on your contract for services rendered to our investors. I suggest you share some of the proceeds if you can.

> *Yours truly,*
>
> *Joseph Arnold*

Willard smiled broadly: Joseph Arnold would not be a problem. Things were going better than he ever dreamed. He already had the last of the remaining cash reserves in hand, which he would use to rent or buy a steam shovel. He would pay the workers out of his own pocket. The timing of the confirmation of the gold strike was perfect. He had no way to contact Arnold about what he had done, even if Arnold caught wind of the gold strike and reappeared. He would move the shovel by railroad flatcar from Eugene through Alvadore, and unload it at Cheshire. Willard was on his own, and in charge.

The Southern Pacific Railroad owned the Alvadore-to-Monroe tracks now, he had heard, and Willard knew that the line was struggling for cash and from unfavorable publicity. He had read with amusement an article about the nearby Mapleton-Junction Highway crossing, which recently had been featured in the Eugene paper. Any train passing through Cheshire was forced to stop at the crossing, whether it wanted to or not. The town's namesake, local resident Lee Cheshire, had gated the tracks due to a property dispute with the railroad. Every passing train had to stop, open the gate, pass through, and then close it. Willard chuckled to himself as he recalled the story on the way back to Eugene. "That's my stop," he said out loud.

Later in the day, he made contact with a Southern Pacific railroad agent to arrange a cash payment to the railroad for transporting the steam shovel, which brought immediate action from the cash-strapped Southern Pacific railroad. Willard hired a shovel operator and arrangements were made to meet him at the disputed Cheshire rail junction where heavy trucks would be waiting. Willard would escort the steam shovel to Horton himself.

Early Wednesday Morning, March 13, 1929

A group of men, including Hiram, Coal, Verin, Gray and Andrew and Joseph Horton, huddled around tables in Molly's boarding house. The third Horton brother, Peter, who managed the lumber sales in Junction City, was also there, having arrived the previous day. Several tables had been pushed together and maps of the old High Pass Road were spread out across them. Railroad workers, waiting for a ride up to the bunkhouse, were milling around inside and outside the boarding house, as were mill workers waiting for the start of their morning shifts. Everyone had heard about the meeting and rumors had swept through town of some kind of discovery up at the crevice. All were curious as to why now, in the middle of winter, there was such a rush to re-open the old road to help finish the west end of the grade. Something was going on, and, of course, they all wanted to know what it was.

"Materials for the trestle bridge at the top have been ready for weeks," someone said. "Why didn't you rush them up there before?"

Stalling to answer, Hiram suggested. "It may be the snow up there that stalled us before." His explanation did not calm the mood of the men.

Finally when questions turned to angry shouts for answers, Peter Horton raised his hand for quiet. "The mill has done its part," he announced, nodding to his brothers, "but the railroad is in financial trouble." The room grew quiet. The Horton brothers stood together and announced to the men that if the railroad could be finished by the time of the seasonal increase in lumber prices, their shortcut railroad had a chance of making it. Otherwise, it would be sold for its salvage value. Opening the old High Pass road was the key. Everyone suspected however, that they had not heard the whole truth.

Finally, when the room became a noisy roar of questions again, Andrew barked out his plan.

"The mill will be closed for a few days," he said. "Most of you will be taken by the old road to the top of the grade to help build the trestle bridge across the crevice. Pack extra clothes and plan to stay in the bunkhouse up there until it's finished."

One of the mill workers protested. "Its no more than a wide cow path. If you plan to travel that road with any kind of equipment, it will have to be cleared. Who's going to do that?" When murmurs of protest swept through the crowd again, Hiram raised his hand for quiet.

"Listen, the old road comes close to the top of the grade in one important place, High Pass crevice," he said pointing to the map. "Additional labor at the top means a quick end to the final half-mile of grade construction as well as the trestle. All the crews can then concentrate on assisting the east side crews to finish their part. They need the lumber and we have it."

When the question came up again on who was going to clear the old road to make the plan work, a voice from the back of the room stunned everyone.

"I will." Willard Spencer had entered the boarding house room and everyone turned and stared at him in silence. Willard's first question was the wrong one. "Where is Bull Kelly?"

It was Hiram who spoke first. "You cheating, big city liar! You're not welcome here!" When Hiram drew back his fist, Verin caught his arm. "Let's hear him out, Hiram, then we'll all take our turns."

"Bull's a-dying, may be dead already," Coal announced.

Willard stood his ground. Thinking quickly, he realized things had changed dramatically. Hiram Jack was very much alive and, worst of all, the Horton brothers knew about the mine and were planning to help finish the railroad with their men. "I'm here to tell you what we got there at High Pass," he stammered, pulling out the assay report from his briefcase.

"We know what we got. We got a railroad to finish in a snowstorm," reported Andrew.

"What we have here, gentlemen and ladies," he said, smiling at Molly who joined the assembly from the boarding house kitchen, "is an opportunity," Willard countered. "The Horton railroad can haul gold ore," he said, holding up and tapping the assay report with his finger, "logs, or lumber down to Bear Creek. I don't much care which. Maybe it can do all three. I'm here to see this thing through." Willard now had the attention of everyone in the room. The mix of mill workers and gandy dancers began talking at once.

"Gold, we'll be rich!" someone yelled.

Willard pressed on, raising his hand for quiet. "No one leave the room!" Willard commanded, as several men were heading for the door, no doubt to spread the word of the gold strike. "No matter what you think of me, the line has to be finished before anybody can make a dime. We can move the ore by rail only if the line is finished. We can all be partners. Equal before the Lord, I swear it. And..." Willard continued, "I brought something we all need."

The rumbling sound of heavy trucks stopping in front of the boarding house caused everyone to look outside. The timing was perfect. The steam shovel had arrived.

Willard removed his hat, tossing it on a nearby table, unbuttoned his shirt cuffs and rolled up his sleeves, like a boxer ready for a fight. It was his moment, and he had to break through to the suspicious townspeople of Horton, somehow.

"Sixty years ago, in 1869, two great railroads and their crews, one working from the East and one working from the West, completed the Transcontinental Railroad. At Promontory Point, Utah, when the last spike was driven, travel across our land went from six months to six days. Now that's what I call a short cut!"

Guarded laughter was sprinkled among the crowd in the boarding house.

"There were hard times finding enough money, there were crews that worked hard and some that didn't. It is the same with this road." Heads nodded.

"Brothers believe! Believe the skeptics that held us back are no longer here. We need only us few to finish. Believe that when we join the lines there will be none like it in the world! Believe in the progress that lies ahead thanks to your hungry hands. Were not true pioneers famished for the future? Who among them would not have built the great railroad; all of them would!"

His voice increased in volume… "Believe that your work from this day forward will never be buried, hollow and unknown when you speak of it. There are cheap elves around that whisper skeptic slop that putrefies in their mouths as they speak; we will carry their stagnant decay no longer.

The dirt bears your signature, here and here…" Willard pointed to the tracks through the window…"the timbers have your temperament in every mile." His voice changed as he let Shakespeare speak for him, from Henry V, the Crispin speech before the battle of Agincourt:

> *This story shall the good man teach his son; on the day we finish it, it shall be remembered.*

> *He that shall live this day and see old age, will yearly on the vigil feast his neighbors, and say, "Tomorrow is Horton Railroad Day.*

The assembled crowd yelled in wild applause.

With Willard's nod of consent, the Horton brothers took control of the meeting. Hiram was voted project superintendent. The rails crew would be split into thirds under the supervision of the three Horton brothers. One group would be given the task of completing the last half-mile of grade as quickly as possible. No more repairs of the lower section would be possible, as time was their enemy. Another crew would begin immediately building Hiram's trestle bridge to the east side of the grade. The men would work in Horton and assemble as much of it as possible, and then the Gentry would haul pieces up the grade to High Pass. The third group would support Willard's steam shovel and the mill crews as they cleared High Pass Road and built a short spur road in to the bridge construction site. The shovel would be needed to dig several steep cut-banks to smooth out the approach to the bridge, and, Hiram suggested, it might also be needed at several spots along Benninger Ridge, on the other side of the trestle bridge.

As sections of the last half-mile of track were finished, the Gentry's load would be gradually increased to see if it could make it to the trestle bridge construction site. If the Gentry couldn't pull the load up the grade, they would have to rebuild the incline of the grade further back down the line.

Willard stood in silence. He was impressed with his performance before the group and the plans that were taking shape. He began wondering how long before the secret of the gold strike would be out. Could this group keep their mouths shut? He doubted it. Thoughtfully, he began thinking about what his next role would be. Then it came to him. When there was silence in the room and the final plan had been explained to the men, he cleared his throat to get everyone's attention.

"If you men can keep the damn secret, I'll get the tracks to you from the east side. By God this railroad is going to be finished!" To Willard's delight, the captivated audience cheered.

"No one is to enter the mine until the line is finished," Willard continued. "Is that clear? Once gold fever hits people, they can turn on each other. I've seen it happen, who knows what people will do. If this is going to work, we need each other. Agreed?" There were shouts of approval and nods from the workers.

For the first time, Willard was feeling camaraderie with the Horton townspeople. The notion quickly passed, however.

"Sheep," Willard muttered, as he left the boarding house. He had several more stops before making the journey to Bear Creek. He would get the workers there to focus on completing the last two miles of the tracks and forget the log unloading station. As long as the secret held, there was still a chance of buying back more shares from unsuspecting farmers and workers on the Bear Creek side.

CHAPTER 22

THE THIRD WAY

The widespread depression in the automobile industry in 1926 led Henry Ford to introduce the eight-hour day and a five-day week. Industrial leaders throughout the nation were shocked. Union leaders thought it was great.

–Earl Kelley, from No Way to ~~Run~~ / Build a Railroad

Wednesday Afternoon, March 13, 1929

Laurie sat with Polly and Rosie in Polly's now-cheerful home. All three were engaged in discussion about a new kind of government. Rosie had no idea what the Distributionist Movement was or a Third Way of living, but, if her mother was interested, she was, too. It sounded great to have more time for herself, for reading and doing the things she enjoyed. The way Laurie explained it, working for yourself was more important than working for someone else. Widespread small businesses and property ownership was part of this movement catching on in Europe and in the United States as well.

Finally, Polly needed to try and summarize what was being suggested. "So," she said, "let me understand this. You're suggesting something different from Capitalism, which is what we have, or Socialism, like they have in other countries, for a Third Way, where everyone works just as hard but for himself or herself, with no central authority. This sounds like a recipe for…" before Polly could finish Laurie interrupted.

"Exactly!" Laurie exclaimed in her excitement.

"What I was going to say is," Polly said, jumping back into the discussion. "It sounds like a recipe for scrambled eggs! Someone has to be in charge. The company here has been good to us," Polly argued.

"Have they now?" Laurie countered, her Irish brogue suddenly audible in her excitement to debate. "This house should belong to you, not the Horton brothers," Laurie added. "Isn't the work Hiram does just like slavery?"

Polly was thoughtful while the question hung in the air. As the two women continued talking about recent events including Hiram's brush with death, "at the hands of the company," as Laurie put it, Polly could see the passion in Laurie's eyes.

Finally, Polly told her firmly, "I couldn't run a small business, I'd have to have help keeping records and making ends meet."

"You're running a business now, in a way; you're running this family," Laurie replied.

"So, you're saying the center of my life should be me, my family, and our needs, rather than the needs of the Horton Mill or the Horton Railroad?" Polly asked, trying again to understand this new way of thinking.

"Exactly!" Laurie said, delighted to hear Polly's continued interest.

"Even two of the Popes, Leo the XIII and Pius the XI, saw the burden of a life directed by oppressive forces like big businesses and interfering governments. They both wrote about it, and about the importance of wealth being distributed among the people in a different way."

"My experience tells me otherwise," Polly said thoughtfully. "We struggled on the farm, even though the girls helped, the farm failed. That was a small business. It was only when farmers band together and stand bigger, that they can manage through the droughts and crop failures."

"The Gentry wasn't made here, remember?" Polly reminded Laurie. "When our homemade truck couldn't pull the grade, we went to a large company in Portland and our company had the Gentry made. There is no way we could have built it or bought it." I think our experiences are just too different to be in agreement," Polly concluded.

"I can see that both are possible sometimes when necessity dictates," Laurie admitted. "I'm thinking of the covered wagons coming to Oregon and the story Verin told my students," she said thoughtfully. "Each wagon had a family that was like a small business. Yet, whenever their lives were in danger, the families banded together into a larger whole for protection. They would put the wagons in a circle for defense. The wagon train had rules too, which everyone agreed to, like following the wagon master's lead and filling up their water barrels when they were told. People had to do their part or the wagon train didn't make it."

"Polly, isn't it true you believed everyone could reach the stars, with the Horton Railroad leading the way? I know that is what you believe; you might as well admit it to yourself. In the end, now, you need more from the mill and the railroad than they can deliver. Don't you see, a dream built by a big impersonal company nourishes them and enslaves your dreams? That's what I am trying to teach both you and Rosie."

"One last thing and then I promise I won't say another word," Laurie spoke urgently. "It doesn't need to be something cold and indifferent like the Gentry next time inspiring you to become a woman of destiny. Can't it just be you, your energy, your creativity using what you have?" Laurie asked. "This is exactly what you've always said you believe. What is best for you, Hiram and the girls is what I want you to believe in, too, that is all I want for you to consider."

"I will think about what we've talked about," Polly said, smiling.

"As will I," Laurie said smiling back.

Suddenly, Willard began knocking on the Jack family's door. He stood there with a rail certificate in his hand. He knew Bull was too ill to deliver one, nor could he remember sending one, following the frenzy surrounding the gold strike. When Polly opened the door, Laurie was standing beside her. Seeing Laurie, Willard took a step back, and removed his hat. Without a word, he handed a large envelope to Polly, turned, and walked away without a word. The women stood in the doorway, looking surprised.

When the envelope was opened, Polly removed the stock certificate and stood gazing at it, slowly shaking her head. It was Laurie that noticed the edges were stained with coffee. "Maybe there's hope for him, she mused. Maybe someday he will give up the top hat."

CHAPTER 23

MATTERS of OWNERSHIP

The Corporation had filed to sell capital stock for $187,500. With Arthur Arnold retaining 51 percent of that, 49 percent of the shares amounting to $91,875 were available for public purchase. How much money from these sales Arthur Arnold received is questionable. But the fact that he did retain 51 percent would have been construed as a vote of confidence in the success of the venture. Until the shares are negotiated, sold or traded, or the company pays a dividend, the stock is of no explicit value. In about a year, Arthur Arnold was gone. How many shares that he held were sold? How much money did he take with him to parts unknown? He had some tough competition to contend with when it came to draining money from the corporate till.

–Earl Kelley, from *No Way to ~~Run~~ / Build a Railroad*

Late Wednesday, March 13, 1929

The Horton General Store had always been the center of community gatherings. It was not only a store and meeting place but also the town's post office. It had burned several times over the years. The Horton brothers had rebuilt the store in different locations around the town. Hopes were high this time that the current structure, built along Swartz Creek, next to the tracks, would afford it some protection against the coming fire season.

A mixture of smells, including an odor of soggy soot, lingered in the entryway of the store. Willard Spencer walked in, quickly surveying the room, the dark, well-worn wooden plank floor creaking under his weight. The store offered a walk through local history. Memorabilia of all kinds decorated the walls: old photos of the mill, mixed in with gadgets, food and household supplies. Without assistance, Willard located the Post Office community bulletin board and posted a notice.

On behalf of the company, he would buy back any shares in the Horton Railroad for a limited time, the notice said, from anyone nervous about the future of the Horton mill and railroad venture. He also reported that shares would continue to be traded in Junction City at their face value, for a limited time.

Willard hoped to keep everyone calm and working while he began mining with the steam shovel. But, with this notice, he accomplished the opposite. He had wanted to speed up his acquisition of more shares from the Horton townspeople, without alarming anyone. His posted statement, stating that the value of the stock certificates for trade in Junction City was limited, worded the way he chose didn't have its intended result. As he re-read it, the sentence wasn't quite right and he was debating how to correct it, when Laurie entered the store, approaching Willard and the notice.

On tiptoes, she read Willard's announcement over his shoulder. She immediately asked him a question. "Mr. Spencer, I would like to know what this last, poorly-written sentence means?"

Willard turned and looked down on Laurie. "Would you now," Willard said, mocking Laurie's Irish brogue. She was much too close, he realized, remembering the encounter at the boarding house. He took a cautious step backwards. He slowly removed his top hat, not feeling any urgency to answer this annoying woman's question. "Please come and sit and tell me how many shares you would like to sell back to the company."

"I don't own any shares in your deceitful company," she replied, irritated at his condescending tone. "You write poorly," she stated.

"This is a routine buy-back opportunity," Willard lied. "The company believes that investors should have an opportunity to change their holdings periodically. I'm sure you've heard the rumors of troubled finances. The company wants everyone to know they can have their money back if they want it.

"I see," Laurie said, as she moved off to another aisle to do her shopping. After shopping briefly she paid the storekeeper and turned to leave. Passing Willard's open briefcase, she stopped. Stamped in large bold letters on an official looking envelope, was a single word, "ASSAY." Glancing first at Willard an aisle away, then at an arrangement of local homemade jams, she snatched the official-looking letter from his briefcase and quickly left the store.

After browsing around the store, Willard seated himself at the only table and sat waiting for customers. Glancing into his briefcase, he noticed the assay report was missing. "That bitch!" he bellowed, startling the store owner. "Where's that red-haired school teacher?"

As Willard quickly gathered his things, the store owner asked, "How long you in town? What do you mean? Your sign says certificates are good for limited time, and I got mouths to feed."

Whether he wanted to or not, Willard had posted a confirming public notice that the wooden railroad was in trouble. Not wanting to answer any more questions, Willard pushed his way out of the Horton Store and strode quickly toward the school.

Laurie read the assay report carefully, sitting at her desk. It was clear there was gold somewhere but the described location was the Blue River Mining District fifty miles east of Horton. Why would Willard Spencer be interested in hard rock mining? Was the company diversifying? Suddenly, she was frozen in place. Of course! The thought came to her in a golden flash. There was mining activity all around them. Had that awful man, Bull Kelly, actually found something at High Pass? It would explain everything, she reasoned: the kidnapping of Hiram after recent blasting, Bull's mysterious injury, a fictitious mine location, and the sudden activity toward finishing the railroad grade in the middle of winter. How many people knew, she wondered. She had to talk to Polly immediately. Laurie burst out of the schoolhouse door and collided with Willard Spencer.

"You're a thief!" He yelled at her.

"You're a thief in a top hat!" she countered.

Willard stepped forward to get his assay report back, grabbing for Laurie's wrists. Retreating, Laurie backed into the glass window in the door to the school, breaking the glass with one elbow. As she struggled to be free of Willard, shattered glass crashed to the floor and scattered in all directions. Mildred Persons, startled by the commotion, rushed to Laurie's side.

"What is this all about, you... you brute!" Millie yelled at Willard. Seeing that Laurie was bleeding, she screamed at Willard. "Let her go!"

Laurie broke free and ran toward Polly's house, dropping the assay report, now spattered with her blood.

"I want this woman fired immediately!" Willard roared at Mildred, as Laurie raced away.

Overwhelmed by the flurry of activity and the sight of blood, Mildred promptly fainted into reluctant arms.

CHAPTER 24

STITCHES

David Hascall   The Longest Wooden Railroad

Friday, March 15, 1929

Retired major Cleve Swancutt, MD, his name shortened to Dr. Swan by some of his hopeful patients, arrived in Horton Friday morning, quite by accident. He had no idea a community of mill-workers lived there; he merely crossed the floating log bridge in search of gasoline for his Model A Roadster. He was further surprised when he drove over the wooden tracks, mistaking them for a cattle guard. His Model A bounced wildly and his right front tire went flat immediately when it hit the tracks, making a loud "bang." The loose rubber from the tire thumped loudly against the underside of the fender and running board. Dr. Swancutt jumped out, leaving his vehicle to coast to a stop on its own in front of the Horton store. Gray came out of the store and ran to see what the noise was all about.

"What kind of town is this, boy, with a cattle guard running down the middle of Main Street?" Dr. Swancutt loudly inquired.

"That's no cattle guard, Mister, those are tracks for the Horton Railroad," Gray replied, proudly.

"Railroad tracks made out of wood?" Dr. Swancutt asked, unconvinced. Turning his attention to his flat tire and then back to Gray, he spoke with an irritated tone. "I need gasoline and a tire repair, it seems."

"They got everything down at the mill, just down the road," Gray replied. "You may have trouble raising anyone there though, on account of everyone is up building the new bridge." Gray stopped abruptly, fearing he had already said too much to this stranger.

"What happened to your chin there?" Dr. Swancutt said, taking Gray's face roughly in his hands, as he studied Polly's needlework. "You tangle with a bear?"

"No…not exactly," Gray replied, sheepishly pulling himself away.

"You still have chunks of dirt under the skin and your lip is misshapen on one side. Who sewed your chin?" the doctor asked.

"Mrs. Jack," Gray replied enthusiastically.

"And where will I find Mrs. Jack? She needs a lesson in doing stitches, boy," Dr. Swancutt stated.

"Up at the boarding house, in the sitting room, tending to the others," Gray reported, pointing up the street.

"Others?" Dr. Swancutt exclaimed. "I wasn't aware you had a hospital here. Take me there immediately," Dr. Swancutt said sternly.

"Mrs. Jack says it's just chunks of the burned log that I fell into. She says in time they will work their way out, " Gray reported, trying to catch up with Dr. Swancutt, whose stride was much longer than his own.

"Someone just took some stitches out and…" Dr. Swancutt said, as he burst through the door into Molly's sitting room. His words caught in his throat when he looked around the room. Coal sat in a chair with a wet cloth on his face, moaning from a headache. Verin sat next to him with his leg elevated on a chair. Bull Kelly was lying on several tables that had been pushed together with pillows under his head and one under his injured foot. Polly was examining the stitches she had just put into Laurie's elbow the day before.

"Who's in charge here?" Dr. Swancutt roared.

"This is my place," Molly said, walking up to greet the newcomer. "But we're full up right now, as you can see."

"I'm Dr. Cleve Swancutt and I demand to know why these people aren't in the Pacific Christian Hospital in Eugene. You can't just pretend to have a hospital in the middle of nowhere; there are rules and precautions!"

Polly stood and turned to greet Dr. Swancutt. "Did the Horton brothers ask you to come and look in on us, doctor?" she asked.

"No, I just happened by, and it's a good thing I did; you have need for a real doctor, I would say, to organize the care of these patients. You've no facility here to take care of them," Dr. Swancutt retorted.

"We make do and use what we have, sir," Polly said cautiously.

"I hardly know where to begin, women just aren't expected to understand how to run a hospital," the doctor complained.

Laurie jumped to her feet. "Sir, are you here to help or hinder?"

"Young woman, I am not accustomed to my patients talking to me that way, in such an accusatory tone. If you want my care please take your seat and wait your turn!"

"Doctor," Laurie began, "you said women just aren't expected to know how to run a hospital. You're wrong! Polly has done a fine job and you obviously haven't heard of Dr. Mae Harrington Whitney Cardwell of Portland, Oregon. She is, for your information, both a doctor and hospital administrator, the first one in Oregon, I believe."

"Well, I don't see her here, so I am in charge," the doctor stated firmly. Dr. Swancutt spent an hour looking at his new "patients." Finally, when it was Bull's turn he needed only a few moments to reach a decision. Shaking his head, he spoke to a sedated Bull Kelly, "If you had come to Eugene, I might have been able to help you. Now, I don't know," he said. "We can watch your foot for another day or so but, I believe eventually, we will have to remove it, Mr. Kelly."

CHAPTER 25

SNOW AND FIRE FROM ON HIGH

David Hascall

Ernest Liska was a high climber. He would limb the spar tree as he climbed, up to 70 or 80 feet, then "top it" by sawing the remaining top off, and as it fell, he climbed onto the top, then as the tree swayed back and forth (12 or 15 feet) rolled himself a cigarette, sat and had a smoke before going back down.

−Earl Kelley, from *No Way to ~~Run~~ / Build a Railroad*

Saturday, March 16, 1929

The Gentry did not return on Friday evening as scheduled. When it arrived on Saturday morning loaded with exhausted mill and rail workers, only a handful of Horton townspeople were waiting. The crews had made little progress during the week, thanks to the 18 inches of snow that had fallen. Numerous equipment breakdowns had occurred, along with a derailment and several injuries. The Horton brothers had met with Hiram at the bunkhouse and it was decided to stop working until the weather improved.

"We have no choice," Hiram concluded.

The steam shovel had been successful early in the week, clearing mud slides off the old High Pass Road, but then the snowstorm had buried the machine up to the cab. Strangely, the town of Horton, less than a thousand feet lower in elevation, enjoyed the start of a mild early spring with warm weather and no rainfall.

...

Willard Spencer planned to make weekly trips to Horton to ensure that work was progressing and see for himself that no one was mining his gold. Under threat of termination, he had worked the crews hard on the Bear Creek side of the grade. He was anxious to see if tracks had reached the mine at the top of High Pass and assumed the trestle bridge was well along in construction. The unloading station, planer mill and log pond at Bear Creek had been abandoned. The last two miles of flat grade were ready for the wooden rails from the Horton mill. Willard intended to get it to them even if he had to truck it around to Bear Creek by way of the Mapleton-Junction City Highway.

Willard had paid a cash bonus to anyone willing to work a seven-day workweek. He intended to make the offer to the Horton crews if necessary, to keep to his schedule. Even though his remaining cash was running low, completion of the railroad was clearly in sight.

He was not pleased, however, with the news from the Horton crews. Most alarming to Willard was the news that buckets of ore had been found in one of the dynamite shacks. When Willard asked to see the buckets, they were empty. One of the gandy dancers had told Hiram that he was sure the buckets had tipped over when the Gentry rounded the Big Bend turn in the grade. Not wanting to accuse any of the men, Willard walked to the Horton Store, hoping to secure more of the stock certificates from unsuspecting ranchers in the Lake Creek Valley that frequented the Horton general store. It would be a good test to see if the secret was holding. There were no customers in the store, so he walked to Molly's for his supper. Perhaps in polite conversation over dinner someone would ask him to redeem their shares in the railroad for cash.

...

While exhausted men slumbered under warm blankets at the Horton Mill bunkhouse and in the town, the long neglected wigwam burner kept sentinel watch. Ashes, more alive than dead, began to stir. The last of the fire's embers, deep within the core of the ash pile, refused to be extinguished. They began glowing blue then pulsated orange and red as waves of unseen air currents played with the outer edge of the flameless debris pile. A panel on the southwest side of the burner, carelessly left open, was providing a draft, the breath to restore the fire to life. Bursts of pitch suddenly popped outward, opening a hole in the pile. Upward, into the darkness the embers climbed, forming lightning-shaped streamers. Strings of curling fire, like golden snakes, poked at the spark screen at the top of the burner; relentless in their efforts to escape. Finally, carried aloft on currents of heated air into the night sky, the sparks rode along on conspiring currents.

No one in Horton saw the fire start.

Sunday, March 17, 1929

At daylight, above Triangle Lake at the southern end of the Lake Creek Valley, Billy Barrows and John Wolfe started their climb. A new patch of timber to be logged meant a new spar-pole had to be made. The limbless tree would support pulleys and high lead cables needed to winch the heavy logs to the steam donkey. The spar-pole had to be ready by the next day. Hired by the Horton brothers, the high lead crew readied their climbing harnesses. Neither man considered himself a thrill-seeker as they considered climbing up toward the top of the 175-foot fir they had selected. The tree, measuring six feet in diameter at the base, was well placed in the center of the soon-to-be-cut forest. Once their safety lines encircled the tree, and they had attached climbing spurs to their boots, the men nodded to each other and began the journey up to a point eighty feet from the ground.

When the tree narrowed to three feet in diameter, they planned to top it. Cutting limbs as they went, they made steady progress, Billy working as the top climber. Both men were able to move several feet at a time by flipping their safety harnesses upward and using the spur points attached to their boots to anchor themselves against the tree. They climbed in a steady rhythm, knowing the other man was near, but not too close to get tangled in each other's gear. Sharpened spurs easily penetrated the bark, holding them in place until the next flip upward of their safety harness. The men carried axes, wedges, a small bottle of kerosene, and a crosscut saw, affectionately called Miss Misery.

At the appointed place, working on opposite sides of the tree, the duo cut halfway through the tree, working the crosscut saw back and forth. After a small cut with the axe opposite the saw cut, a small puff of wind caused the men to stop their work. The top of the tree gave an audible "crack" in the still morning air. Without a word, John retreated down the tree a few feet opposite the side the top was predicted to fall. The men held their breath waiting for the wind to die down. The wind was unusually warm for this time of year, they agreed, but it was always their enemy. It kept the men frozen in place and watchful. Finally the wind grew quiet.

Nodding to John, Billy cautiously continued undercutting the treetop, widening the wedge-shaped cut he had made with his axe. With every swing of the axe, he would glance downward, not to the ground but at John. One word from John that the top was moving would bring a stop to the undercutting and an immediate swing away from the treetop if it fell toward him. The axe, with the rope safety line attached, would be allowed to fall to his side. The most dangerous part of the tree topping was beginning. Billy had to hold onto the tree below the cut with all the strength he could muster. Another puff of wind and the treetop began its earthward journey. Billy heard the only word he needed from John. "Down left!" John yelled.

Billy immediately dropped his axe, pulled both spurs from the tree and leaned into the tree giving slack to his safety harness. Sliding down the tree a few feet, he jammed both spurs back into the tree to break his descent. Stopping a few feet above John, the treetop was falling exactly as they had planned. "Damn, we're good," Billy said excitedly, looking downward with a grin. Both watched as the treetop fell to the forest floor to land with a loud crash.

Both men held on as the sturdy, top-less tree began to arc, recoiling in a wide circle, now free of its top. The men watched the forest move around them, enjoying their swinging ride at the top of the spar-pole. Around them was a sea of treetops, their domain in the Lake Creek

Valley—their brief kingdom at the top of the world.

Looking east to the snow-capped mountains above Horton, they could not believe what they saw on the horizon. John pointed toward the sunrise that had just begun. "What do you make of that?" Two suns appeared to be rising in the early morning light. Then the men looked at each other—realizing what they were seeing. One of the red glows was billowing smoke. Horton was on fire.

CHAPTER 26

THE AWAKENING

Three times during the period of building the railroad, the Horton mill burned, and twice they rebuilt. Those costly interruptions in the production of railroad building materials, combined with the lost construction time, must have been aggravating almost to the point of insanity.

−Earl Kelley, from *No Way to ~~Run~~ / Build a Railroad*

Sunday Morning, March 17, 1929

Following a healthy dose of aspirin and laudanum administered by Dr. Swancutt, Bull Kelly had slept well. He felt somewhat better. Dressing before daylight on Sunday, he hobbled into the doctor's room very quietly and removed the bottle of the opium-based painkiller which he found on the doctor's night table next to his bed. Quietly leaving Molly's boarding house, he disappeared into the hazy, predawn darkness. The air seemed smokier than usual, but he had no interest in investigating.

Bull woke up Coal and told him that he needed help to retrieve the ore buckets from the dynamite shed, he said, so he could, "leave Horton with something."

"I'm in trouble and that Sawbones wants to take my foot," he told Coal. When Coal told Bull that the dynamite shack was empty and so were the buckets, Bull swung his improvised crutch at him. In the ensuing struggle, Coal pushed Bull out the front door of the mill bunkhouse and down the steps. Noticing the heavy smoke coming from the mill, he left Bull lying at the bottom of the steps and ran to investigate.

Scout's repeated nervous nickers from outside aroused Tara in the predawn darkness. With only one eye open, she walked to the window. A solid yellowish-red glow in the distance caught her attention. At first, she thought it was the sunrise. In the middle of her second yawn, it dawned on her that it was in the wrong place. She suddenly realized the Horton mill and several of the nearby buildings were burning, sending shooting flames high into the air.

Racing to her parent's bed, Tara stood in the doorway and screamed, "Fire!"

Running back to her room, she awakened Rosie, too, and together the girls quickly dressed in warm clothes. Tara ran out of the house to check on Scout and Rosie followed. They made their way down the hill toward the Horton store to see if they could help.

Laurie was sound asleep when loud voices and heavy boots outside her window woke her. People were racing by the room she rented at the back of Molly's boarding house. Fearful and cautious, she put on her coat and slowly opened her door. She could see smoke drifting toward the Horton store and the schoolhouse. Men were racing toward the mill, quickly disappearing in the smoke. Hazy blue-black smoke hovered just off the ground. As she dressed hurriedly, she searched her room frantically for anything to help put out the fire. Grabbing her water pitcher and chamber pot she ran to the schoolhouse.

Willard Spencer had slept fitfully. The pounding on the door to his room startled him; he sat up, struggling to come to alertness. This disturbance better be good; he thought. Quickly putting on his trousers, he lifted his suspenders over one shoulder and opened the door. Molly was standing there. She thrust a zinc bucket into his stomach.

"Everybody helps! We're burning!" she yelled. "Throw water on everything you can."

"What?" Willard stammered.

"No fire department here, big city boy, everybody helps," she repeated excitedly. "No exceptions for top hats!" Molly rushed down the hall to the next room in her boarding house.

Willard retreated to his room and slipped his shirt on under his suspenders, cursing as he went. After putting on his shoes, he made his way outside, in no particular hurry. People appeared to be running every which way. Smoke from the burning mill shrouded the whole town. Judging by the chaos he saw in the street, no one was in charge. Choking and coughing repeatedly, he filled his bucket in Swartz Creek and began to walk toward the mill.

The first building he could see through the smoke was the schoolhouse. On the roof, he could see the red-haired schoolteacher precariously hanging onto a ladder, throwing water on the roof. When Laurie retreated down to refill her water pitcher and chamber pot, Willard was standing there and raised his bucket for her to grasp. It took a moment for him to realize what he had exchanged his bucket for.

At that moment, it did not matter that he was the man she most despised in the world. She took the bucket from Willard and headed back up the ladder without a word. When she returned, Willard had refilled her pitcher and was waiting. The chamber pot had mysteriously disappeared into the depths of Swartz Creek.

Quoting a favorite poet, she said, "The pitiful among men is he who turns his dreams into silver and gold."

"What?" Willard asked.

Laurie didn't answer and was already climbing the ladder to continue wetting the wood shake roof of the schoolhouse.

Well after daylight, all three Horton brothers stood shoulder-to-shoulder watching the fire. The rapid progression of the flames had surprised them. Their faces were red with fatigue and shock. Their mill would be a total loss. A dozen neatly stacked piles of freshly cut lumber burned like torches around the outside of the main buildings. As one pile of lumber burst into flames, the pile next to it began to smolder. Within minutes, that pile would spontaneously burst into flames. There was no longer a way to reach the mill with the burning lumber piles all around it. The fire was so hot; the brothers continued to move back as each new pile caught fire. Even though Swartz Creek flowed by the mill, there was no fire control system to put the water to use.

When the smoke began to dissipate and the fire raged no longer, Laurie climbed down from the ladder. Willard sat, exhausted, on the schoolhouse steps, the site of their previous conflict. Laurie sat down beside him. "I'll be a thankin' you now, Mr. Spencer. Bein' you helped me save the school."

Willard gave her a long gaze. "The people here work hard," he said. "Harder than anybody I know. They deserve what's in the mine up there," he said, pointing at the tracks leading out of Horton.

"What the people have here, Mr. Spencer, is a place to belong to," Laurie said. "They believe in Horton and themselves. We need each other to make it, no matter where we come from."

"I don't belong to this place," Willard spoke thoughtfully. "I believe in profit and possibilities."

"And on whose back would you gain those profits, Mr. Spencer?" Laurie asked.

Willard did not answer. When the last of the swirling smoke made them cough at once, they looked at each other and both stood. Laurie smiled at Willard then quickly walked away toward the boarding house. When Laurie was some distance away, Willard called after her. "I don't think you belong here either."

Neither of them saw the Gentry as it slowly moved past and out of sight up the grade. Loaded on Saturday night, the lumber cars carried the last of the precious wood planks and engineered beams needed to complete Hiram's trestle bridge. Smoke in mysterious swirls shrouded the cab of the Gentry; there appeared to be no one at the controls. Anyone watching would have concluded the train was simply being moved away from the fire for safety. The only clue to the identity of the engineer was a spray of tobacco juice that came from the cab, as it made the turn at Big Bend and started the climb to High Pass. Bull's destination was the dynamite shed. He was sure Coal had lied to him because he had stranded him in the mine.

It had been relatively easy to coax two young passengers aboard the locomotive, in the supposed interest of "their safety."

CHAPTER 27

THE MISSION

Was this a foolhardy senseless venture? Not in my opinion. Had the demand for, and price of, lumber held up; the railroad would have been successful.

—Earl Kelley, from No Way to R̶u̶n̶ / Build a Railroad

Late Morning, Sunday, March 17, 1929

G ray Palmer was the first one to notice that the Gentry was missing. He had caught up with Hiram on the path leading back to their hillside home. Hiram had stopped and was surveying the damage below, slowly shaking his head. He began pointing out the damage to Gray as he stood beside him.

The Horton store looked untouched except for a section of the roof that had burned through. The bare, blackened rib-like rafters were visible with the store's contents exposed. The sound of hammers and shouting could be heard below. Men were still arriving from the southern end of the valley to survey the damage and lend a hand. A fire at this time of year had been unexpected.

The Horton Mill had been reduced to a pile of charred rubble. The wigwam burner, however—the cause of the fire, appeared untouched. Nearby homes had also escaped the flames, although several woodsheds had been reduced to ashes as were the wooden tracks leading to the mill, the mill bunkhouse and a newly constructed outhouse. The smoke from the mill continued to pour into the sky but flames were no longer visible. Hiram was already thinking about the railroad and the loss of the rail lumber for the last stretch of grade at Bear Creek. He was lost in thought until Gray broke his concentration.

"Who took the Gentry up the grade, Mr. Jack?" Gray asked.

Hiram shrugged his shoulders and shook his head as the two of them walked up to Hiram's house. Polly had filled every container in their house with water from their spring and was waiting for news. She was immediately wrapped in her husband's arms, burying her head in his chest.

"We were not so lucky this time," Hiram reported. "The mill and the bunkhouse are gone," he said. "I don't know what to think, what will we do now for rails to finish."

Seeing Gray, Polly gave him a brief hug. "I think Dr. Swancutt is still in town," she said. "He may want to take a look at your chin. You're going to have a scar, Grayson. Maybe he can do something about it," she said sadly, examining Gray's face. One side of his lip remained misshaped, and she feared other scars would remain as well.

"Where are Rosie and Tara," Gray asked, wanting to change the subject away from his injury? "I think Scout threw a shoe, when I was up the grade the other day. I forgot to mention it."

Polly turned to Hiram, "I thought the girls were with you?"

"I didn't see them in the smoke, I thought they had come home. I'll go find them," Hiram said.

At that moment there was a knock on the door. Laurie stood at the front door and knocked, "Can I enter the surgery?" she asked.

Gray quickly left, feeling self-conscious about his face. Hiram was right behind him. At the doorway he turned to Polly, "Gray said the Gentry is missing, but how far can a train get on a dead end track?" Hiram said, trying to lighten the mood.

"The school is saved but the Horton brothers say the railroad can't be finished now," Laurie began from the doorway.

"I'm afraid we are headed into desperate times, Polly," Laurie surmised, sadness in her voice. "Everything alright up here?"

"We are fine," Polly replied, as she moved a washtub filled with water to her sink, preparing to empty it. "We are surrounded by desperate men, like Willard Spencer. I don't think he can be trusted. He will light-out and leave us the way Joseph Arnold did...now, for sure," Polly said.

"He helped me save the school though," Laurie reported and the two women exchanged surprised expressions.

"Well, that's something," Polly replied.

"If only he could feel something for Horton, the way we do. He doesn't really have a home to believe in. His life is hollow like an empty seashell," Laurie said, thoughtfully. "The Third Way is the only alternative for people like him to become who they can be. Big Business caused him to be this way. That is the real disaster," Laurie said finishing her thoughts.

"Perhaps, Laurie, perhaps," Polly said. "Fire caused the mill to burn today however, not the Horton Brothers, or the railroad people. We live with the risk of fire all year long, as you can see. To me this disaster is unfortunate but we will recover and be stronger than ever.

"True," Laurie said. "Dependence on the lumber mill however, created false hope in the railroad; that is the disaster that is here now and will be here from here on, Polly," Laurie stated, defending her position. Polly could only nod her head. Something else was nagging at her. The girls had still not come home.

Hiram had asked several people around the Horton store, but no one had seen the girls. He began to worry. Gray was right, the locomotive was not in town and there were only a few men who could start the Gentry, or for that matter, move it once the engine was running.

Molly was busy mopping the floor of her dining room. Countless boot prints outlined with soot had made visible tracks everywhere and she was sweating profusely from her labor. Hardly pausing to answer his question, she shook her head. Tara and Rosie had not been in the boarding house that morning. Hiram was now alarmed. Not finding Bull at the boarding house either, he decided to check Bull's company house. On the way, he ran into Verin and asked him to check the house with him. He explained that his girls had not been seen since the fire that morning.

"It's probably nothing, but it is strange," Hiram said, "Someone moved the Gentry and its loaded cars out of town as well during the fire."

Inside Bull's house they found a message painted on the wall that shocked them both.

> *"I mean to have my gold. I found it first. I'll blow that new big trestle if anyone comes near. Tell Jack, I got them girls. Teach you, for my misery."*

Hiram sank to his knees, both hands covering his mouth, a fearful expression contorting his face.

"Mother of God!" Verin exclaimed, "The man's gone mad." They both ran from the house. Verin limped quickly toward the mill to find the Horton brothers. Hiram raced home.

Polly and Laurie sat, stunned at the news. Hiram did his best to comfort Polly, but she would not be comforted. Without warning, she ran to the corner, removed the blanket from Hiram's trestle model and began smashing it with her fists. When Hiram restrained her, she began kicking the model. Only when he pulled her away did she stop. Suddenly, she turned to face him and began striking his chest with her fists.

"You brought us here! You get my girls back," Polly ordered.

Hiram did not say a word. He released his grip, grabbed his coat and hat and began to leave. With tears in his eyes, he stopped at the doorway as Laurie spoke. "It's not going to be this way," she said with authority. "Whatever it takes, Hiram, you get your girls back."

Hiram nodded; without saying a word, he walked back over, gently kissed Polly on the head, and left the house.

CHAPTER 28

INCHING UP TO HIGH PASS

David Hascall

The workers performing this task of a standard construction practice had no fear of their mentality being brought into question. These were all structures born of necessity, with the accepted inference that they were for temporary use; the normal life span being limited to the length of their need. Necessity is a common motivation for innovation.

−Earl Kelley, from *No Way to ~~Run~~ / Build a Railroad*

Monday Morning, March 18, 1929

Tara had become unmanageable, and Bull had grown weary of the energy it took to keep her from jumping off the Gentry, so he locked both girls in the dynamite shed near the Big Bend turn in the grade, previously occupied by Gray and Verin, and continued on his way. They would get free soon enough, but Bull was pleased with himself. The grief he would cause Hiram Jack was some solace at least, in "payment" for the pain he had suffered from the knife wound.

Near the top of the grade, he encountered snow, but the Gentry responded eagerly, and pushed it out of the way. Bull was impressed with how far the crew had gotten without him. The tracks were just short of High Pass Crevice. He was glad not to have to walk the last half-mile to be near his gold mine. He limped to the dynamite shed that had been filled to the roof with buckets of ore; mined by his two previous "partners," the deceased Seymour Purvis and Hiram Jack. The door was open and the shed stood empty. That double-crossing Coal, Bull thought. He has all the ore buckets.

"Everything I've worked for is gone!" he muttered. He felt renewed anger and a desire for quick revenge toward his most recent partner. If he ever saw Coal again, that partnership would also end the way Seymour's had, he thought, nodding to himself. An evil sneer crossed his face. Everyone here was against him now.

He looked back down the grade to see if anyone was following him. Something was important about the grade here but he couldn't decide what it was. He shook his head to clear his thoughts.

Eager to get back to the warmth of the Gentry, he had to hold tightly onto the stair railing leading to the cab, as he paused to wait for dizziness to pass. Even in his weakened state, however, he realized what his mind had been wrestling with. One big question had been answered: as he looked at the full load of wood trestle beams and planks coupled behind the Gentry, he smiled. "She's a logger," he said out loud. "She can pull the grade with a full load."

Hiram paced back and forth as Verin remained seated at his kitchen table, his leg elevated on a pillow. They agreed that, with the provisions in the bunkhouse near the top of the grade, Bull could hole up there for some time.

"You know I have to go after him, he has my girls."

"I know, but no telling what he will do," Verin said. "You're going to need all the help you can get. I'm no good to you with my leg; it's still no account. I would only slow you down. And, the Horton brothers and their crew are bogged down with their mess at the mill."

"They tell me they're not rebuilding this time," Hiram said. The two men looked at each other, each realizing the project now faced nearly impossible odds.

"Maybe it can be finished with the wood from the spur lines," Verin suggested. "Take the wood that is already in use and move it. The spur to the bunk house, a dead-end parking spur and the turn-a-round shouldn't be needed much longer," Verin suggested.

Hiram nodded. "I thought of that, too. The Gentry can run either way on the rails: I know that, it has a reverse gear. There still may not be enough for the last two miles to link up Bear Creek," Hiram said dejectedly. "We can try to make the wood stretch. There may be some wood we rejected along the way somewhere."

"Take Gray with you," Verin offered, changing the subject back. "He's a lot like you, good in the woods, too. Maybe a might head-strong, but he's been an easy keeper for me since his folks died of that God-damn flu." Verin paused, deep in thought.

"I'm thinking you might surprise Bull if you hike up the old High Pass road. He don't know the road's been partially cleared by the shovel. You might be able to get the high ground on him and see what he's up to."

Hiram nodded. "How about I get the Banks brothers to help comb the grade from here for the girls," Hiram said thoughtfully.

"Every one of them boys comes with a rifle, wherever they go," Verin said, cautioning him. "You sure you want to take a chance on one of the girls catching a round in a cross fire?"

Both men were silent for a few seconds. Gray walked into the house at that moment, having completed his evening chore of milking Verin's Jersey cow. The cow had stepped in the bucket of fresh milk and swatted Gray across his face with its tail. Gray's chin was hurting, and his anger surprised the men as he stomped to his room, slamming the door.

"Gray?" Verin called, ignoring his show of emotion. "Get your hunting pack. You're taking a hike up the High Pass road with Mr. Jack, here."

Gray came out of his room quickly, still visibly upset at the loss of the milk. "Damn that cow!" he yelled.

"I know," Verin replied. "Ruined the milk again, didn't she. You were in a hurry; pulled on her teats too hard. She don't like it. Now listen up," Verin instructed. Gray was still shaking with anger.

"Let it go, Gray, I need you to help Mr. Jack, here."

...

Rosie and Tara were alone in the dark dynamite shed. Tara had kicked at the door until her foot began to ache, and then slumped to the floor, sobbing. Rosie tried to comfort her, putting her arm around her shoulder. Tara was angry, as well as hurt, and pushed Rosie away. "That man is a bad man!" Tara shouted. "Papa never told him to save us from the fire. Now we're stuck here!"

"We can think our way out of this, " Rosie said calmly. "Come on now, let's try. We can make a game of it," Rosie said excitedly.

Monday Evening, March 18, 1929

Polly and Laurie were restless. Hiram had been gone all day, without any word reaching them. The two women had eaten their dinner together at Molly's, lost in silent thought. Molly had joined them trying to offer some comfort. The three women sat looking at their partially eaten bowls of stew.

Finally, Polly broke the silence. "The girls will be hungry now," she said. No one spoke. "Shall we help you tend to these dishes?" Polly asked.

"How long do we wait before we go look ourselves?" Laurie asked.

"Hiram can find them, I know he can," Polly answered.

Hiram and Gray had stood by the shovel near the top of High Pass. The giant piece of earth moving equipment was hopelessly stuck in the snow.

"I want you to drop back down the road a mile or so and cut cross-country 'til you get to the tracks," Hiram said. "I'll go on across here to the crevice and see what Bull is up to. If you find the girls, take them down the grade to their mother," Hiram insisted. "Don't wait for me."

"Bull is somewhere along the grade though," Gray objected.

"With his foot like it is, he won't go too far from the bunkhouse or the Gentry," Hiram said. "Don't let him see you, Gray, if you can help it."

"I think he intends to blow something up," Hiram continued. "There is no telling what that madman will do. If you don't see anything, work your way up the grade, and I will meet up with you along the tracks, on my way down." Gray nodded in understanding.

"And, Gray," Hiram added, as the two parted company, "one more thing: if you decide to stay out all night, go to one of the sheds for shelter. There was a lot of scat along the road walking in here," Hiram said, grinning at Gray. "One bear story is enough for you, I would guess. If we don't meet along the tracks, no need for you to come looking for me, you hear? We need to find the girls."

Gray walked briskly back down the High Pass road, excited and fearful. Within a few minutes, he cut down hill and cross-country toward the wooden tracks. The hillside was slippery and soon his overalls were muddy from slipping on the steep, snow covered slope. He stopped, removed his pack and gazed across the canyon that lay before him. He realized one of the wooden trestles was at eye level from where he stood, hugging the hillside on the other side of Swartz Creek. He scanned the trestle from one side to the other looking for movement along the tracks. Next, looking down, he realized he would have to cross the fast-moving creek to get to the grade.

He had nearly drowned not far from here just a few days ago at the hands of Bull Kelly. He swallowed hard, blew out a ragged breath, and began to look for an easy way across. As he searched for a shallow crossing, he noticed movement along the creek. He sank to his knees to try to remain hidden.

A long maple tree limb stretched part way out from the bank, extending more than halfway over the swollen stream, but it was not sturdy enough to be any use to him. However, its noiseless swaying movement interested him. The branch dipped into the high water in perfect rhythm, as if pushed by the hands of an unseen oarsman. Silently struggling against the flow, the limb would be swept downstream by the current, then rise on its own strength and lunge back upstream to its normal place. Gray stood watching it, feeling that it was waving for him to come closer. His eyes moved downstream beyond the limb to an old-growth Douglas-Fir tree. It had fallen the entire way across the creek, high up on the bank. Crossing there would be easy.

Bull became preoccupied with the realization that the tracks were being completed all around him as he could plainly see, without him. Trees and tracks were all becoming his enemies. Walking to the edge of the crevice, he had trouble focusing on the tracks, which now looked like they had been completed up near the crevice from the east side of the grade as well. Were the tracks moving? Was someone there? His mind was playing tricks on him, and he was confused and filled with indecision.

Removing the rickety bridge and a trestle would keep them all away from his gold mine. Someone was trying to take his gold by taking advantage of him in his weakened state. But, without the bridge he would be trapped too, his escape made more difficult due to his injured foot. Am I already trapped, he asked himself?

Bull began to breathe rapidly, walking in circles. It took a few moments for his thinking to clear to realize that his walking made the pain in his foot worse. A brief moment of clarity in his thinking returned. Only two miles of flat section remained to be built down below, not here. He had seen all of this before. Suddenly other thoughts flooded back into his mind. A twisted realization came to him with a jolt. "These farmers are going take my gold from both sides if them boys build the crevice trestle," he said out loud.

If Hiram Jack got his girls back, the pain he's been sufferin' is still not enough, Bull thought. Thoughts of further revenge began to seethe and settle inside again; thoughts that were easier to hold onto. Everything else was becoming hard somehow. The last of the Dilaudid he had stolen from Dr. Swancutt was gone, and he was out of chew.

Bull began to walk in circles again, trying to decide how to heap more revenge on Hiram Jack. Suddenly, with the dizziness returning, he stopped. Looking back down the wooden tracks and at the cars coupled behind the Gentry, the next desperate steps came to him. "Blow it all up, the bridge beams, the Gentry and a trestle," he said out loud.

"Mr. Jack," he said, addressing the trestle beams stacked on the first car. "No one builds a grade like Bull Kelly! Your trestle will soon be kindling."

In an unusual moment of clarity, it dawned on Bull that Hiram had several reasons besides his girls to come after him. Only two other people knew the exact location of the mine. Hiram was one of them. The fool would come for his precious girls, his trestle wood, and the gold.

"You come," Bull sneered. "Just me and you now," he said out loud, carefully opening the box of the only thing he had found in the shed, a box of dynamite.

Rigging the lumber cars behind the Gentry with dynamite gave Bull a distraction from the constant throbbing in his foot. He uncoupled the cars from the locomotive, after settling on the placement of the charges: under the middle lumber car. Fumbling and cursing as he went, he started the locomotive and considered his next step. His knees felt weak, and he caught himself as he nearly fell out of the cab of the Gentry.

He would light the fuse and push the cars with the Gentry back down the tracks toward Horton. The dynamite would blow somewhere down the line. If I am lucky, Bull thought, it will explode on one of the larger trestles and take it down.

If he could make it down the East side of the grade, he was sure to find someone who would look after his wounded foot. No one would know anything about the girls or the explosion for days. Inflicting pain on anyone who might take his gold was all that mattered.

Hiram had crossed the short distance through the forest from the High Pass road, trudged through the snow to the crevice and had been watching Bull for some time. The man was clearly mad he thought, as he watched Bull walking in circles. When he saw Bull open the box of dynamite, he nearly gave his presence away, jumping to his feet. He could not see his girls anywhere and figured that they must not be nearby.

Bull lit the fuse on the lumber car and turned to hobble back to the Gentry, its motor idling in readiness. Hiram was waiting, an old fury returning. Hiram struck him a glancing blow over the head with the only thing he could find, a short rail plank from the construction site. Bull sank to his knees immediately. Hiram stood over him, ready to strike again.

"Where are my girls?" Hiram shouted, raising the board.

"Back down the grade," Bull mumbled defensively, raising one hand to deflect Hiram's next blow. "Locked in a shed there, safe enough," Bull said, his head hanging down to his chest.

Hiram did not see the knife that Bull removed from his pocket with his other hand. It was Coal's knife, the one he had used to injure Bull at the edge of the crevice. Fumbling to open the blade, Bull tried to stand.

When Hiram swung the board again, Bull was able to deflect it and get to his feet with the knife blade open. Bull lunged at Hiram, cutting his arm deeply, halfway between his elbow and wrist. Hiram staggered backward, wincing in pain.

As the two men faced each other, Hiram noticed that the lumber cars had rolled away on their own, without the weight of the Gentry holding them back. Hiram retreated to the cab of the Gentry for safety, his arm bleeding profusely. Bull followed, looking up at Hiram from the tracks, a satisfied smile spreading across his face. His head hurt, but Hiram was cut, and the cars were on their way back down the grade, a full case of dynamite strapped to the middle lumber car.

Hiram struggled to find reverse in the cab of the Gentry. The large geared lever was difficult to manage with one hand. Finally, the Gentry started moving backward down the grade following the lumber cars. Hiram bound his arm with his handkerchief to stop the bleeding. The gash from the knife had opened a jagged flap of flesh that had to be held in place while he bound it tight and adjusted the speed of the engine. As the locomotive went by, Hiram could hear Bull ranting between bursts of laughter. "Foot for an arm, pain for pain, we're even now."

As darkness began to fall, Gray was crossing a long trestle over Swartz Creek, just below one of the dynamite sheds. He felt the wooden tracks under his feet begin to vibrate. At first he was hopeful that Hiram might be coming, driving the Gentry that would carry them all safely back to Horton. When he realized it might be Bull driving the Gentry, he broke into a run. He had to get clear of the trestle or be knocked off by the Gentry as it passed.

Out of breath, Gray rested just off the end of the trestle. The train's lumber cars rumbled past. When he realized the locomotive was missing, he knew something was very wrong. Suddenly, there was a deafening explosion that knocked Gray to the ground. The night sky lit up with streaks of fire and billowing black clouds, the air suddenly filled with choking smoke. The lumber cars were midway across the trestle Gray had just been on when the dynamite had exploded. Many of the trestle timbers under the lumber cars simply disappeared. A deep rumbling sound echoed out of the canyon below, as the cars derailed, one by one, and plunged downward into the canyon. Gray regained his feet and watched in horror.

When the explosion's echo reached Horton, Polly and Laurie were trying to convince Verin to join them in the search for Tara and Rosie. The women wanted him to drive the company car as far as possible up the High Pass Road, even through the snow and let them join the search, using the car lights and horn as a signal. Verin had reluctantly agreed to drive them up, but only as far as the snow line and then back to Horton.

Gray was dazed and in shock. Down in the canyon, after the explosion, the remaining wood for Hiram's trestle bridge burned fiercely. Gray began staggering along the grade, now in the dark. His head was buzzing, and he was so dizzy, he was unsure where he was. Staggering forward, he fell between the tracks and lay on his back. When the trees around him stopped spinning, he sat up. Firelight reflected off the trees around him. Ahead, the metal sides of the dynamite shed reflected a strange red, silvery glow in the moonlight. The building appeared to be burning, too, as waves of smoke danced and played with the colors from the burning trestle timbers in the canyon.

There was something he was supposed to do here, but in the shock of the explosion, he couldn't remember what it was. Only when he heard Tara's whimper from inside the shed did he realize where he was. He had found the girls.

"Tara, that you? Rosie, you in 'thar?" Gray asked. Shrieks of recognition came from inside the shed, startling Gray, making him jump to his feet. "Where you at," Gray asked. "It's dark out here."

"This side, this side, hurry," he could hear Rosie saying. Prying loose a board near the door and working together by feel, the three of them soon stood, hugging each other along the wooden tracks. At that moment, the tracks again began to vibrate. "He's coming back," screamed Tara. "That awful man is coming to kill us." The three of them shuddered, frozen with fright.

"There's no way down the grade," Gray told them. "The trestle came down with the explosion. The Gentry will go off the end and down into the canyon." When the headlight of the Gentry came into view, Gray could only think of one word to say. "Run!"

Hiram was barely conscious. It had taken a long time, but he had driven the Gentry slowly down the grade, aware that the wooden tracks ahead might have been destroyed in the explosion. He had stopped and checked every shed along the grade for Rosie and Tara. Bull may have lied, he concluded. Hope of finding his girls—along with his strength—was fading in the inky black darkness.

The Gentry had been easy for Bull to follow, although he moved slowly, painfully. Each time it stopped, Bull got closer. He kept cursing Hiram to himself as he struggled along. Hiram was stopping at all of the sheds. The fool doesn't know which one of them the girls are locked in, Bull thought, a wicked sneer on his face. With each new wave of pain, one thought kept him going: reduce the number of men who knew about the gold mine by one more. Just one more stop and he would catch up, surprise Hiram and finish the job with Coal's knife. No one would suspect him of another murder.

The Gentry stopped in front of the shed where Tara and Rosie had been held captive. Like the other sheds, no one was here, and Hiram's hopes sank. Curious, Hiram thought. In the back up light of the Gentry, he could see that the door on this shed was locked, yet one of the boards near the door had been forced open. Hiram's heart began to beat faster.

"Tara, Rosie," Hiram yelled as loud as he could. "Gray, it's Hiram."

When he turned to yell the other direction, back up the grade, a large figure came out of the shadows behind the Gentry.

"Oh, God," Hiram yelled, as he looked into the smiling yellow teeth of Bull Kelly.

Suddenly, Hiram was on the ground, struggling. Bull had wrestled him down and was sitting on his chest. Hiram's arms were pinned by Bull's massive grip. Bull was fumbling with Coal's knife, trying to open the blade.

Hiram kicked furiously, making Bull's task difficult. "Hold still, damn you! My gold mine, my gold mine," he kept repeating.

Out of the darkness, there was a flash of movement, a violent collision, and a grunt from Bull, who flew off of Hiram. Tara had returned and had delivered her best greeting. She rolled off the startled Bull and jumped to her feet. "Papa!" she yelled.

Gray and Rosie appeared out of the darkness and helped Hiram to his feet. "He's a bad man, Papa," Tara yelled at Bull, who lay on the ground, his wind knocked from him, gasping for air.

"Gray, quick find some rope in the Gentry tool box under the seat," Hiram ordered. "Girls, come here and help me with my arm."

When he climbed into the cab of the Gentry, Gray easily found the rope. He couldn't help noticing the whistle cord that dangled before his eyes. He reached for the cord with a broad smile on his misshapen face. The blast from the Gentry's whistle startled everyone and could be heard all the way down to Horton.

The blast from the Gentry whistle after dark was, "a good sign," Verin said, after the explosion they had heard. Both sounds had rippled down from High Pass, bringing townspeople out of their houses. Polly and Laurie had come running out of Verin's cabin, at the edge of Horton. All three paced back and forth along the tracks waiting and trying to make sense of first the explosion, followed by the Gentry's whistle. The sounds drew Andrew Horton, who roared up in his company car and joined them.

Leaning out the car window, Andrew sounded doubtful as he reported, "The whistle sounded faint and far away, near the bunkhouse I would say. The explosion sounded closer; don't know what to make of it. Sound does funny tricks in the dark."

After an hour, when the Gentry didn't appear, Polly and Laurie insisted that someone take them in the car as far as possible up the old High Pass road. The lights are a beacon in the dark," Laurie suggested. "If someone had been hurt in the explosion, they'll find us."

"Maybe the whistle was a call for help," Polly suggested.

"If Bull blew up a section of the track, it would be difficult to continue down the grade in the dark," Verin volunteered, nodding at Polly's idea.

A hastily assembled supply of blankets, bandages and water were packed into the Chrysler and soon all four were headed up the old road. Bumping along in the dark, it took them several hours to reach the shovel.

"Would have been faster on foot in the daylight," Andrew growled as he set the hand brake and shut off the engine. "How long we going to stay out here?" he asked, looking at Verin.

"We're not going back tonight," Polly reported, irritated at Andrew's impatience. "My girls are out there!"

"We didn't see anyone on the road," Verin reasoned. "That means they're all over on the grade, Bull too…likely staying in the bunkhouse or in one of the dynamite sheds 'til daylight. That's what I would do."

"Then at daylight I'm going over to the grade," Polly said emphatically.

"You're putting yourself at risk if you go over there without an…" searching for the correct word he finally settled on "…escort," Verin cautioned.

"Escort yourself back to Horton then," Laurie said angrily.

"Now ladies, I can't walk that far, and Andrew here needs to keep driving the road; maybe they will cut across from the grade at daylight and show up. We need to stick together in case someone needs mending, Polly."

CHAPTER 29

THE LAST STOP

I used to go and watch the men work, building the railroad. One morning I rode my bike up to where they had been working the day before, and there was no one there. The tools were all laid out, the material and everything was there, it's like they stopped to go to lunch and never came back. They never did.

— Ernie Smyth, in *No Way to ~~Run~~ / Build a Railroad*

Tuesday Morning, March 26, 1929

At daylight, over the objections of both men, Polly and Laurie stood at the edge of the crevice looking across the rickety bridge toward Benninger Ridge. They had insisted on searching for the girls themselves, leaving Verin and Andrew to drive the road. Following Hiram's frozen tracks in the snow, they found High Pass Crevice easily. No one was there. The muffled sounds of men working drifted up toward them from the east side of the grade. Polly and Laurie could hear horses and shouts from somewhere down the ridge. They were both cold, and huddled together, as they stood, watching down the ridge toward Bear Creek with intense curiosity.

"Maybe someone is coming up from Bear Creek to help with the search?" Polly suggested. "Maybe one of them has seen the girls?"

"No, I hear hammers and tools working," Laurie said slowly. When it was full daylight, with their eyes squinting into the eastern sunrise, they could not believe what they were seeing. A line of wagons loaded with trestle timbers, rails and grade ballast was moving away, back down the High Pass Road toward Bear Creek. Workers appeared to be taking the railroad apart, no longer finishing the remaining section on the east side of the grade.

Polly filled her lungs with the damp, cool air, shaking her head. "I don't understand! What are they doing?"

"They don't know about the mine, no one told them," Laurie said. "Maybe Willard didn't pay them." She could feel herself becoming angry at the thought of the deception. "The railroad was built all this way, and won't be finished," she said, shaking her head in disgust. "They are taking it all down to Bear Creek, for what?"

The question hung in the air as Polly strained forward at the edge of the crevice, checking the other side of the rickety bridge for her girls. "Tara! Rosie!" she called, her voice echoing down toward Bear Creek. "Are you there?" After listening carefully, she turned back toward Laurie, and spoke thoughtfully. "Building materials, barns and fences," she muttered. "You use what you got and make it last, make it do or do without," she said, repeating Hiram's words.

"I guess you can't blame the crews," Laurie said, as the two walked side by side. "They owned the land, remember, traded it for shares in the railroad. They probably feel they own the wood too."

"Hiram hoped for more than this," Polly interjected. "I did, too. It isn't right, Laurie. I'm telling you it just isn't right."

"They have heard about the fire and know the railroad can't be finished, I'm sure," Laurie said thoughtfully.

"Soon there won't be anything left," Polly said, defeat evident in her voice.

Laurie placed a reassuring hand on Polly's shoulder. "We have hard times now, thanks to men like Willard Spencer, not these men," she said.

"I don't think they know what they're doing." Polly added. "They are farmers not railroad men, after all. A railroad man would never do this," she added, dejectedly. "Hiram's dream will never be built," Polly sniffed, holding back tears. "Some short cut."

On impulse, Polly grabbed a rock, turned and drew back her arm, nearly hitting Laurie. She threw the rock as hard and far as she could across the old crevice bridge. She threw another and another until her arm ached. When they heard angry shouts directed toward them, they turned and walked a few steps down the west side of the grade and out of sight of the crevice.

"I think a lot of things will change now," Polly said dejectedly. "We will be poor, and Horton will never be anything but a ghost."

"You believed in this company Polly," Laurie said, "…the mill, the railroad, all of it. I don't think I ever did. People knew I wasn't a believer, and you can see how Spencer treated me as a result."

"He could tell you were suspicious of the company, that's what a lot of people feel about you, not just Willard Spencer. They didn't understand where your loyalty lay," Polly said. "Everyone here works for the mill or the railroad. They have to believe in what the company is trying to do. Why would anyone stay here if they didn't believe? Everyone respects you, Laurie, make no mistake about that. Willard Spencer has no respect for most things, and most people, especially women. People here need you, too; the kids need you," Polly said encouragingly. "People overlook things when there is respect and when they need each other. That doesn't make the company wrong, or you right."

"Did anyone every say you don't belong here, or your ideas just won't work here?" asked Polly.

"No, they didn't, " Laurie agreed. "No one except Willard Spencer. After the fire he said he didn't belong in Horton and neither did I." After the two women walked for a while, Laurie stopped suddenly. "Sometimes I was excluded, though; that's almost the same thing. For instance, no one asked me to help at Hiram's service."

"Yes," said Polly, "I remember, I requested that you not be asked to help. I didn't understand your special interest in my Rosie. When I realized I wanted you to teach me about the Personalist movement and the Third

Way along with Rosie, I was confused and Hiram was still missing. I think I just wasn't ready. Now with the railroad failing, the mill burning, and my kids missing, I am trying to make sense of who is responsible." After searching down the grade for several hours and then around the bunkhouse, Polly began to feel hopeless. "If I have lost my girls over this, I will never forgive the Horton brothers or my husband for their part in this folly, that's for sure," Polly said, threateningly. "The Gentry will be Horton's albatross and not a symbol of anything that's good."

They began the walk down the grade to Horton. After walking silently for a mile, Polly gave a big sigh, as if exhaling thoughts that no longer had a place. She stopped and took Laurie's hand in hers, kissing it gently. They walked on hand in hand.

Polly did not let go of Laurie's hand until they were startled by familiar voices coming from down the grade ahead of them. They ran forward, quickly crossing one of the many curved trestles that hugged the hillside along the grade. As they rounded the bend in the wooden tracks, they saw the girls.

"Rosie! Tara!" Polly yelled excitedly. "Thank God, you're safe!" As the girls rushed forward, Hiram and Gray broke into a run right behind.

Polly and Hiram stood facing each other with the girls sandwiched between them. For a brief moment the cold morning air was forgotten. Hiram could read Polly's lips that silently said, "Thank you." When she saw Hiram favoring his injured arm, heavily wrapped in a makeshift bloody bandage, she released the girls and gently inspected it. "I see my grade master needs mending again."

"Where is the mad man?" Laurie asked.

Hiram and Gray looked at each other. "Tied to the Gentry," Gray said, "he always said it was his."

The End

INTERNET SOURCES

Geography of Horton; Topographical maps

http://www.topoquest.com/map-detail.php?usgs_cell_id=21163

Gold in Oregon History

http://www.coinsite.com/content/faq/20gold.asp

http://www.oregongold.net/tag/lucky-boy-mine/

The Bohemia Mining District

http://bohemiamineownersassociation.webs.com/history.htm

Historical Gold Prices

http://www.wisegeek.com/what-is-the-historical-price-of-gold.htm#lbimages

History of Fire in Oregon

http://www.oregon.gov/ODF/Pages/fire/sb360/wui_history.aspx

High Lead Logging

http://content.lib.washington.edu/curriculumpackets/logging/index4.html

http://www.osha.gov/SLTC/etools/logging/manual/yarding/example_systems.html

Mapleton-Junction City Highway

http://en.wikipedia.org/wiki/Oregon_Route_36

Men of Inspiration

http://en.wikipedia.org/wiki/G._K._Chesterton

http://www.english.illinois.edu/maps/poets/m_r/markham/markham.htm

Oregon Mineral history and management BLM

http://www.blm.gov/or/programs/minerals/

The Economy of the 1920s

http://www.huppi.com/kangaroo/Events1920s.htm

http://www.thepeoplehistory.com/1920s.html

The Third Way Movement

http://en.wikipedia.org/wiki/Distributism

http://en.wikipedia.org/wiki/Third_Way_%28centrism%29

Transportation by rail

http://www.oregonencyclopedia.org/entry/view/oregon_
electric_railway/

http://www.accelerationwatch.com/promontorypoint.html

Women of Inspiration

Willa Cathers

http://www.123helpme.com/business-of-farming-in-willa-
cathers-o-pioneers-view.asp?id=162920

Dorothy Day

http://en.wikipedia.org/wiki/Dorothy_Day

Abigail Scott Duniway

http://www.wikipedia.org/wiki/Abigail_Scott_Duniway

Mae Harrington Whitney Cardwell

http://oregonencyclopedia.org/entry/view/cardwell_mae_
harrington_whitney_1853_1929_/

Irene Ware

http://en.wikipedia.org/wiki/Irene_Ware

Women's Suffrage

http://bluebook.state.or.us/facts/scenic/suffrage/suffintro.htm
http://teacher.scholastic.com/activities/suffrage/history.htm

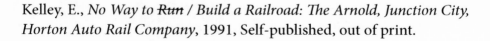

BIBLIOGRAPHY

Kelley, E., *No Way to ~~Run~~ / Build a Railroad: The Arnold, Junction City, Horton Auto Rail Company*, 1991, Self-published, out of print.

History of the Lake Creek Valley, compiled by Mary Benninger Minter, genealogy compiled by Elma Sprague Rust, for the Horton Lady's Aid Society, 1968 and 1973.

Appendix

Although we no longer have orphanages in the United States, in other countries however, they continue to exist, often serving those who created them more than the children that are institutionalized. Thanks to the attention given to children at the turn of the 19th century by then-president Theodore Roosevelt, and Progressive Movement leader Jane Addams, the movement to aid dependent mothers and children took hold in the United States. The White House Conference in 1909 entitled, "The Welfare of Children Conference," the first such event hosted by an American president, provided the fuel for change. Progressive Movement leader Jane Addams would later become the first American woman to receive the Nobel Peace Prize for her humanitarian efforts. The reader is referred to the following link for a jaw-dropping history of the orphanage system in this country.

The Rise and Demise of the American Orphanage—Johns Hopkins

www.jhu.edu/jhumag/496web/orphange.html

We continue down the road to a complete transformation in the care of all vulnerable peoples, with the reform of the health care system in the United States. However, we are moving painfully slowly, beset by those who fear the very infrastructure that removed the old and destructive orphanage system.

The reader must keep in mind that many countries lag behind the Shelter Home and the Foster Care System present in the United States, due to a lack of political will or lack of infrastructure resources.

What makes the Good Shepherd Orphanage of Guanajuato, Mexico, special for me is that it is more than an orphanage providing food and shelter for children. It serves as a school, church and sanctuary for mothers in crisis. It is a facility teaching hope, in a world that prefers raw materials for manipulation.

One of the Sisters and a few of the children of the Good Shepherd Orphanage are pictured. None of the mothers agreed to be photographed.

Hiram's application to work on the design for the Golden Gate Bridge, secretly mailed to San Francisco in the winter of 1929, depicted the bridge that is shown here.

Loaded log car that may have ridden the wooden rails
to the Horton mill

ABOUT THE AUTHOR

David Hascall has lived in the Pacific Northwest all of his life, and grew up in an area similar to the town described in this book—albeit a few years later than when the story takes place.

David has been a registered nurse and health educator for 40 years and a Certified Diabetes Educator for 15 of those years. While employed at Sacred Heart Hospital, he was the first nurse to perform hemodialysis treatments on patients with chronic kidney disease in Eugene, Oregon in 1975. He holds two masters degrees and currently works for Agate Health Care in Eugene. His early jobs included working in the fields of bean growers near Eugene, and he holds a self-proclaimed record of the most pole beans picked by hand in a single day: 653 pounds.

He lives with his wife Barbara in Eugene, Oregon, and his two children are now grown and on their own. David can often be found at Eugene's Saturday Market helping in his wife's soap, lotion and body care products booth. His hobbies include cycling, Oregon football, fishing, travel, woodworking and cooking for friends. This is his first book.

Final thoughts from the author:

> *There is a destiny that makes us brothers: None goes his way alone: All that we send into the lives of others, comes back into our own.*
>
> *—Edwin Markham*

David Hascall   The Longest Wooden Railroad

EPILOGUE

The twin **Key** brothers, preachers in the Pilgrim Harvest church got the start they were looking for with the miracle at the Horton School. They planted 13 churches in the Lake Creek and Willamette Valleys over the summer of 1929; a torrid pace they were sure would net them control of the Western Region of the Pilgrim Harvest churches. The number thirteen proved to be unlucky however, as the stock market crash that year forced an end to the ministry. Many of the churches survived, reorganized under other denominations. After the loss of their flocks, and out of money, the brothers decided to try their luck at gold mining. After praying for several hours they chose a recently abandoned gold mine. The Lucky Boy mine, as it was known in its heyday, had been the largest mine in Oregon. Located at 4500 feet on the McKenzie River drainage, the mine never made them rich but gave them an excellent view of the heavens on a clear night.

A rumor circulated throughout the Lake Creek Valley late in 1929 that **Preacher Earl** had an excellent view of the flagpole from the front of the classroom during the service for Hiram Jack. Looking through the glass window in the schoolhouse door, he had simply made a lucky guess that the ragged man standing there was Hiram Jack. Was it truly an act of the Lord? Few in Horton accepted the rumor, but there were those who did. Many of the disbelieving visitors who flocked to the classroom, left smiling, shaking their heads at the cleverness of the Keys brothers.

Mildred Persons lived for 2 more years; insisting until her dying day that her fainting at the memorial service for Hiram Jack was a response at being overcome by the spirit of the Lord. Falling into the arms of Andrew Horton, her "good friend," was viewed as quite convenient. Mildred, an author as well as a teacher, was in the midst of assembling a recipe book when she died suddenly. Her work was finished by a multitude of women from the Lake Creek Valley as a memorial to her.

The **eight Banks brothers** who left the unmarked bear trap that caught Verin Palmer the night of the search for Hiram Jack, gave up trapping in the woods above Horton after the incident. They became quite good at distilling corn liquor, leading hunting parties up the grade and peeling Chitum bark.

Bull Kelly escaped from his rope bonds and disappeared into the mist of the Oregon Coast Range.

Toby Coalanski (Coal) successfully obtained half the mineral rights to the High Pass Crevice Gold mine, as he was one of only two people who had actually set foot in it. The mine, registered as the "Gentry Lady," continued to produce a small amount of color for several years, but not enough to rebuild the railroad. After working the mine on behalf of the Horton brothers, Coal sold his interest to them and moved to Junction City. As payment, the Horton brothers traded Coal one of their prized possessions, the Gentry. Coal moved the engine to Junction City along with a number of ore buckets that suddenly reappeared. Portions of the Gentry can be seen today in the back of the Junction City Historical Museum. Coal became quite good at restoring railroad cars and train whistles.

Hiram and Polly Jack lost their company house in a second fire started by the Horton Mill's Wigwam burner in the fall of 1929, one of the driest years on record. Polly insisted they move to Eugene. In 1932, Hiram proposed deepening the millrace in Eugene; long used to provide water for steam power generation. His plan to increase the flow levels to facilitate electricity generation was ahead of its time. The Chambers family never adopted Hiram's plan, owners of the millrace.

His employment application to work on the design for the Golden Gate Bridge, which he secretly mailed to San Francisco in the winter of 1929, was never answered. A picture of his design can be seen in the appendix.

Laurie Flanagan also moved to Eugene where she successfully started the Woman's Auxiliary in 1930. Among her many noteworthy achievements was the cleanup along the Willamette River, near the old site of the Eugene Water and Electric Board. After Hiram died in 1949, Polly and Laurie moved in together. They were instrumental in the process of getting Hiram's beloved Millrace recognized as a national historic industrial site. Their efforts were finally rewarded in 2003, long after both women had passed.

Joseph Arnold made one last appearance in Horton in early spring of 1929, after receiving a message from Bull Kelly: Bull had been right about the mess at the Bear Creek work site. Arnold sat in the back of the classroom, the last person arriving at **Hiram Jack**'s memorial service. Believing that Bull Kelly was responsible for the disappearance of one of his silent partners in the railroad project, **Seymour Purvis**, he had come to investigate. In his car he drafted a termination letter, following the report of Bull's kidnap of Hiram Jack. In the letter he appointed Hiram as the new rail superintendent. He left the letter with Laurie Flanagan, whom he had never met previously, having been unable to find his other silent partner and favorite schoolteacher, Mildred Persons. His letter was never delivered; the Horton brothers had already named Hiram to the position. Arnold's grand vision of an eighteen-mile wooden rail shortcut to the Willamette Valley came just two miles short of completion.

The **Hult family** would fulfill his dream of getting the Lake Creek Valley timber to market using log trucks, over the newly improved Mapleton-Junction City Highway (Highway 36) and High Pass Road, only a few years later. **Joseph Arnold** had the right vision, just not the means. Years later, in 1962, one final mention of Joseph Arnold is found. He is given credit for naming the "Mohawk Rocket," the locomotive for another Willamette Valley privately owned logging railroad.

Willard Spencer left Eugene in the summer of 1929. He had gambled everything he had, as so many did that year, and lost it all. He had just enough money for a one-way train ticket to San Francisco, and as he loved animals, began working at the San Francisco Zoo cleaning stalls. Laurie Flanagan's chamber pot often came to mind.

Grayson (Gray) Palmer and Rosie remained lifelong friends. Gray moved to Eugene following the death of his grandfather in 1936, and served as a conductor and finally as an engineer on the Oregon Electric Train system serving Eugene, Portland and Salem, until the line closed in 1945. He often thought of his adventures along Swartz Creek as the railroad line swept along the Willamette River between Eugene and Portland. He kept in contact with the Jack family for many years. He returned to Horton and tried to become a writer. Only one minor published work can be found.

Tara Jack started a back-country guide service in the Oregon Cascades, the first of its kind in Oregon owned and operated by a woman. Following the death of her pony, Scout, in 1940, she would often disappear for months at a time into the Three Sisters wilderness. Her last known address was the Taylor Burn Guard Station in the Willamette National Forest.

Rosie Jack moved to Boston and became a nurse. She never returned to Horton.

The three **Horton brothers** and their families continued on in Horton. Andrew became the town's first Post Master. His brothers each started their own fraternal organization and all three continued to be active in the school system they had worked so hard to improve.

THE END